XT JL pg. 17

THE LUCK
OF THE
SPINDRIFT

THE LUCK
OF THE
SPINDRIFT

A Novel of Adventure by

MAX BRAND

DODD, MEAD & COMPANY · NEW YORK

ISBN 0-396-06470-1
Library of Congress Catalog Card Number: 72-175310
Printed in the United States of America
by Vail-Ballou Press, Inc., Binghamton, N. Y.

THE LUCK
OF THE
SPINDRIFT

CHAPTER 1

Samuel Pennington Culver, Doctor of Philosophy, never used the titles he had acquired at Harvard and the Sorbonne because he was a man who did not believe in useless ornament. He considered himself a person of eminently practical mind; nature had bestowed on him, he felt, the glorious gift of a mind to use, and the wretched handicap of a body to support. For that support he had to work eight hours a day, and to fight off decrepitude or the danger of illness he spent another hour in exercise. It was his body, again, which demanded six hours of sleep. On the whole he considered it an unhappy bargain that required fifteen hours to meet physical needs, and left him only nine hours for his books. His chief quest was a search for a key to the Etruscan language, some Rosetta Stone which he might decode and so give to the world the buried mind of that great people.

Samuel lived in a small room that overlooked a backyard surrounded by a high wooden fence and bright with laundry on Mondays. To the east, through a slot between two buildings, he had a glimpse of San Francisco Bay and the blue, feminine curves of the Berkeley hills beyond; but the distances he yearned for were not those that feet can wander through; and most of his time at home was spent seated at his corner table, where the light from the window streamed over his shoulder—or beside his reading lamp.

He worked at night for an express company, his task ending somewhere between one and three o'clock in the morning, after which he walked briskly up the hills from the waterfront, ran up the stairs to his room, threw off his clothes, slipped into his bed, and was asleep the instant he closed his eyes. That was because he never permitted himself the luxury of sufficient rest. Six hours after he closed his eyes, a pin-prick of conscience roused him. He rose at once and commenced the hour of exercise which kept doctors and doctor bills from his way of life. At thirty-five his body was still garnished with exactly the same two hundred pounds of lean muscle that had caused the college football coach to yearn after him. Having finished this task, Samuel Culver bathed, dressed, and ate the breakfast which in the meantime had been simmering on the gas stove in the corner of that tenement room. After this, Samuel sat down to his books. He remained with them for eight hours and twenty minutes.

Books, in fact, filled his friendless existence as utterly as God ever filled the life of an ascetic hermit. Once a year he was compelled to buy clothes for the sake of common decency; otherwise every penny he saved from his steady work and his monastic spareness of living went into new volumes. Nearly three thousand volumes were now within the walls of that small room.

If Samuel Culver had a friend in the world, perhaps it was that doddering old bibliophile James McPherson, who kept the second-hand bookstore and watched the market to find items for Culver; and the only pleasure excursions that Culver took into the world were among the musty stacks of books in the shop of McPherson. Only the day before, he

2

had gone with his month's savings to McPherson and come away with Diodorus Siculus in a fine old edition. Jolly Diodorus! What a credulous fellow he was! Culver, at his work, could not help chuckling and wondering how he had got on so long without the old fellow.

As he chuckled, the sharp, hard lead of his pencil was running rapidly over the paper, putting down the names and addresses which Tommy Lester called from outside the little glassed-in booth where Culver sat writing out the labels.

It was after eleven and the night's work promised to be short, so Samuel Culver already was foretasting the happy return to his studies. He breathed more deeply of the savor of the air off the Bay, but his eyes never shifted from the pad over which his pencil flew.

"From T. W. Langer," intoned Tommy Lester, "Eleven forty-nine Haight Street, S.F.; going to Mrs. Randall Scott, Nine eighteen Franklin Avenue, Fruitvale. It's a parcel—"

The pencil was flying over the address of Mrs. Randall Scott, when Culver's spectacles slid off suddenly, as though a sudden gust of wind had jerked them. Vainly he caught in the air to save them. They slithered off the tips of his fingers and left him to fumble in the obscure mist in which, without his glasses, he lived.

Touching the floor, he felt rapidly across its surface. Outside the window of the booth he could hear the stifled laughter of Tommy Lester, and knew that Tommy, with a reaching fingertip, must have played the trick on him. Now his hand found the glasses. He arose. His head banged heavily against the writing shelf. He stood up, vaguely peering out the window at the dark cavern of the warehouse. All was blurred, as though he were looking at a scene under sea. It was high time, he felt, to give his eyes that rest recommended by his doctor. He rubbed the bump on his head as

3

he readjusted his glasses.

"You shouldn't have done that, Tommy," he said. He had a mild voice, low-pitched and musical.

"Shouldn't've done what, you mug?"

Culver considered Tommy steadily; he had to use a surprising effort of the will to master a desire to lay on hands. Then he was able to say: "Go back to the Randall Scott address, if you please. I've forgotten what followed."

"Watch yourself!" whispered Tommy. "Here comes the old dope himself!"

And now Culver saw "the old dope" in person, standing in the truck runway. Channing floor-bossed the whole warehouse. He had a bad leg, and went about with two canes to steady a weight that was increasing every year faster than his salary. By sheer luck, as he stood now at watch, the horn of an approaching truck, as it swung around the inside turn, blasted the ear of Channing. He had to move with undignified speed to get out of the way, and Channing's dignity was his greatest possession. That was the moment when Channing heard Samuel Pennington Culver say again: "Go back to the Randall Scott address."

That was when Channing exploded. He eased his way into a speech that began: "The Randall Scott address? To hell with the Scott address! What's your address? You inside, there—you, Culver, what's your address? You may not know where the Scotts live, but do you know your own home number?"

Tommy, as he listened, shrank his head down between his lifting shoulders and squinted his eyes, as though he were facing a biting wind. Culver, on the other hand, leaned out the window and studied Channing with intense interest. With such a voice Achilles must have shrunk the waters of the Scamander and loosened the knees of the frightened Trojans; with such a voice old Rustum had thundered by

4

the Indus when the sword of Sohrab had wounded him.

"A blow is about to fall," said big Samuel Culver to himself, "and apparently it is to strike me." Meantime, he made careful note of the parted lips, the shaking jowls, the bulging eyes of Channing.

"Yes," said Culver, "I know my home address."

"Then why in hell don't you use it?" bellowed Channing. "Leave Randall Scott—leave everything, leave me, leave the whole damned company, and get out. And don't come back. If you know your way home, go there and stay there."

"The language of passion," said Culver, pleased to the smiling point. "I discover that it is rhythmical. I'll leave as soon as I've made a note of your speech."

And pulling out the notebook which always was with him, he wrote in it with his quick pencil; then he stepped outside as the floor boss cried: "Rhythmical? I'll rhythmical you, you four-eyed flat-foot. Get out!"

"Personal abuse—passion—rhythm. Extremely interesting," said Samuel Culver, and wrote again in his notebook.

The red flower of anger faded suddenly in the face of Channing.

"Clean batty!" he muttered, and swung himself away on his two sticks.

Culver looked up to find a disconsolate Tommy staring after the boss.

"I'm going after him," said Tommy. "I gummed it, and I'm going to tell him what I done. Why didn't you bluff it through? Why'd you have to stop and ask questions when that dope was right here in our hair? Damn your glasses, anyway," groaned Tommy. "How would I know it would knock hell out of everything if I gave them a job?"

He set his jaw and started after Channing, but Culver's big hand stopped him.

"You stay here with your job," he advised. "I've only myself to think of; and you'll have yourself and your wife on your hands."

"Have you saved up some dough? Are you O.K. till you get a new job?" asked Tommy, biting his lip with anxiety.

"I'll do very well," answered Culver.

"You're a great guy!" broke out Tommy. "You're the greatest guy I ever knew! Listen, big boy—by God, I'd go to hell for you!"

CHAPTER 2

Culver walked out of the warehouse still enchanted by his discovery that the language of passion is indeed rhythmical—until he stepped into the street where the wind was blowing billows of San Francisco fog, a dankly penetrating mist. Under foot the pavement sweated with glistening blackness, and the whine of the wind joined together the whistles of two ships in the Bay, big-throated horns that gave to the air a mournful vibration rather than a sound.

Culver shook back his shoulders, but unhappiness would not fall from them. With his fingertips, he counted the eleven dollars and odd cents with which he had been paid off. He walked on, surprised by the coldness in his heart; it was the fear of the unknown. . . . He found himself on an unfamiliar street corner and paused there to take his bearings.

Automobiles in a continual stream carried their headlights up the hill, casting their white halos before them, lurching across the level of the cross street, and sliding smoothly on. A horn began sirening in the middle of the lower block, an urgency in the sound that pushed the foghorns on the Bay into a hushed background.

From the seclusion of his thoughts, Samuel Pennington Culver regarded the hurried urgencies of the world with a sad amazement. Into that atmosphere of jump and bustle he would be forced to stop, now, in order to find new work.

He realized, now, that he had come up a block too far, but instead of turning at once toward his home, he remained to watch for an instant the cross-currents of the traffic. The lights changed; the east-west automobiles roared an instant in first, shifted up to second, and lurched out over the level of the street crossing, the car of the loud horn accelerating far faster than the rest.

Behind it a dark silhouette developed, bobbing up and down in the mist, laboring over the rise, and now developing into the vague outline of a dog that strained at the full bent of its strength. On the near side of the cross street it overtook the car whose horn was already sirening again, and leaped for its running board, slipped, rolled outward on the street, rose with cat-footed speed again as an eastbound automobile struck it a glancing blow that rolled it like a tumbleweed into the opposite gutter. As for the car at which the dog had jumped, Culver saw it sweep on up the rise of the hill. He could see only the man beside the driver with the glow from the street lamps brushing dimly over him. He seemed to fill the automobile with his bigness. His profile was faintly sketched, but it seemed as hard as stone, with a jaw thrusting out like a fist, a huge beak of a nose, and the suggestion of a cruel smile. . . .

The dog lay in the gutter with blood on his head. His bulk dammed the small trickle which ran down the hill, pooling the dirty water; his tongue, creased as though with scars, lolled out into the pool. Culver lifted the big head.

It was a surprising weight. The head of a grown man could not have been heavier. But he was huge all over, with

7

forepaws almost as big as a doubled fist. A pelt of thick gray fur, loose as a lap-rug across the knees, covered the bones and rippling muscle beneath.

Culver saw that blood continued to drip from the head wound and knew that life remained in the great body. He lifted the dog from the gutter instantly to place it on the sidewalk. The head sagged down. The loose weight tried to spill from his arms like jelly. He had to hold the dirt and slopping wetness of that burden close to his breast; and as he did so a strange warmth began in the heart of Culver, flowing outward through his body. They were two outcasts, two discards. From that instant it was impossible for Culver to abandon the big fellow.

At that moment the lights halted the east-west traffic, and Culver strode hastily across the street, the great dog in his arms. He had two blocks to go before he reached his house, but he made the journey without a halt. He climbed the front porch of the rooming house, laid down the big beast while he fitted his key to the lock, then took his derelict back to his room and laid the wet body on his bed.

Turning toward the stove in haste, his leg struck a pile of books. Seven volumes of Ovid spilled across the floor. Epictetus and Lucretius lay unregarded in the fallen column; for the first time in thirty years, books meant nothing to Culver, as he got to the stove and lighted the gas. He filled the saucepan with water and placed it over the flame.

With a towel he rubbed down the dog vigorously; and still the brute, almost as big as a man as it sprawled on the bed, remained inert, with closed eyes. Half a dozen times his hand anxiously sought for a reassuring heartbeat.

It was a triangular, jagged wound that penetrated the scalp of the dog, how deeply he did not dare to probe. With hot water he washed the wound; with iodine he cleansed it more deeply, and as the pungent stuff entered the raw of the flesh, he heard a deep-drawn breath; the whole body of the dog shuddered violently, lay still again. But life was there. Culver cut some adhesive tape into thin strips and with it closed, with delicate fingers, the mouth of the wound. After that, he could think of nothing else to do except to sit on the bed beside the dog and stroke its head, particularly the leonine wrinkles of thought between the eyes. As his hand moved, rhythmically, words came mechanically to his lips. The meaning was not present in his mind as he repeated over and over again that fragment from great Sappho in which she describes, with her voice of music and her divine simplicity, the ending of the day that brings the sheep to the fold, and the child to its mother's arms.

While his lips still moved with those famous words, he was trying to think out the problem. The dog had been pursuing through the night either a friend or an enemy. No friend, surely, could have failed to stop his automobile when the poor brute reached the side of the car and was knocked headlong in the traffic the next moment. Yet Samuel Culver recalled the urgent haste with which the automobile had been driven; perhaps there was some mission in hand so vital that the life or death of a dog was as nothing by the way. This was a possible explanation. But when all was done, there was the picture of that grim fellow in the front seat. Once seen, he could not be dismissed. There came to Culver a foreboding that the man would enter his life again.

Something moved on the bed as swift as a striking hand. It was the head of the dog, and his teeth closed over the forearm of Culver between the wrist and the elbow, while the big brute gathered his legs beneath him as though preparing to spring. His eyes were on Culver's throat.

Instead of defending himself, Culver put his free hand on the head of the dog and continued stroking, keeping rhythm with the lines of Sappho. Sweat from his forehead ran into his eyes, but he continued the stroking and the sound of his voice; if the spell broke, he would have that fighting devil at his throat in an instant! Now, by small degrees, the pressure across his arm was relaxing. The big dog with a sudden movement jerked his head back and held it high to study the face of this new man. There were depressions in the fur behind his ears and across his face. That was where the bars of a muzzle must have chafed.

This high lifting of the head had made a gap between them and broken the current, as it were; and now Culver moved his hand slowly to cross the chasm. The upper lip of the beast instantly curled up from the teeth, flaring out the black nostrils. A snarl of murderous promise ran up the scale; the vibration of it set the bed trembling, but Culver kept on extending his hand. He was half minded to reach for the brute's throat and try to batter his head against the wall, but a far stronger instinct urged him to continue that quiet battle of will against will. Yet it was not a battle, either, but rather an attempt to bridge that gap, a million years wide, between man and beast.

The dog drew back his head like a snake ready to strike. The fur on his throat and breast bristled. But the hand of Culver reached him. And Culver could feel the shudder of the whole body under his touch in a complete horror of revulsion. Still the teeth remained bare, the snarl continued; but he felt that the electric connection between his brain and the brain of the animal had been established again by that sense of touch.

CHAPTER 3

The morning light and the pin-prick of his conscience wakened Samuel Culver from a dream in which he had solved triumphantly the Etruscan language.

He remembered that he had something other than study before him, on this day. He had to start out on the pavements to find a new job. Now, at last, he might have to accept work as a translator, even if the rate were only twenty cents a page. Or perhaps he could find some sort of task as a laborer. At this thought his future brightened for him instantly. For if he worked as a common laborer, perhaps in the street, he would get exercise in plenty without having to use a precious hour out of every day in keeping that body of his in a healthy condition.

Stretching and yawning, he turned his head—and saw, against the slowly shifting white of the morning mist, a great dark silhouette pasted against his window. It was not a silhouette; it was a living creature. And now the full recollection of the evening's adventure returned suddenly upon him. He stood up from the bed. The dog, shrinking as it turned its head, favored him with one brief snarl. Then it resumed its study of the blankness of space as the fog drifted past.

All those hours of the night preceding had not established an amity between them, but rather a state of armed truce out of which battle could be precipitated by a single hasty gesture. As for the rapid movements of his setting-up exercises, it was plain that Culver could not indulge in them while this package of emotional dynamite was in the room as an audience. At that, it probably was hungry dynamite! He dressed, and hurried down to the little corner market.

Mr. Farbenstein was greatly surprised.

"Hai, Mr. Culver!" he said. "What are you wanting at this hour?"

"Meat," said Culver.

"Meat!" cried Farbenstein, amazed—for Culver never bought meat.

"Perhaps not," said Culver. "But what else would you feed a dog?"

"A dog? You have a dog to feed?" cried Farbenstein. "What kind of a dog, please?"

"Something bigger than a police dog, but somewhat that wolfish type. Much bigger."

"Well, feed him dog biscuits."

"Dog biscuits?" murmured Culver. "I don't think so. Raw meat, I should say."

"I'll grind it for you," declared Farbenstein. "How many pounds?"

"Two at least. Good meat, if you please."

"Yes, yes!" cried Farbenstein. "Good meat for the dogs of good people! How I can tell people by the things they buy is nobody's business, it is so wonderful. I don't need to read the mail of this neighborhood; I only watch their grocery and their meat orders. That is enough. Next to what the laundryman knows, the grocery store is what can tell your mind from day to day."

He got out the meat, weighed it, and began to push the cut-up scraps into the grinder. The electric motor sent through the shop a deeply vibrating sound that reminded Culver of the dog's snarl. . . .

As Culver, returning, opened the door of his room, the dog whirled from the window and leaped at him. Recogni-

12

tion stopped that attack before it was driven home. On braced legs, the big fellow skilled to a stop. His first reaction still gave him the mask of a green-eyed devil.

Culver unwrapped the meat, squatted back against the door, and offered a morsel of Mr. Farbenstein's best in the palm of his open hand. The dog pricked his ears, sniffed, and then lifting his head, he looked across the room toward the window as though food were entirely beneath the dignity of his attention; he was betrayed by a thin streak of saliva that drooled down from his mouth. Culver smiled and waited.

Hunger is a great bender of dignity. The big dog turned his head once more toward the meat. He seemed to find a mystery in the close association of Culver's hand with the meat which it held. His nose, constantly sniffing, seemed to draw him forward against his volition. But long minutes went by, and the extended arm of Culver ached to the shoulder before the big head darted out and the fangs nipped the meat cleanly away. The dog, recoiling as though from danger, leaped away half the length of the room.

But there was another morsel in the hand now, and the scent of fresh meat laid hold on the very vitals of the dog. He could not help slipping near again. Perhaps there was a memory of the night before, when a strange warmth of kindness had passed from those same fingertips into the whole body of the dog. At any rate, he ventured in and with a wolfish side-slash of his teeth clipped away the red meat again. It was not so clean a job, this time. A tooth-edge had split the skin of Culver; his own blood was kneaded into the next lump of meat which he offered. And the dog, with that added scent in the air, began to snarl as he worked his cautious way closer.

When blood is drawn, there is a fight. What could be a more elemental rule than this? Culver knew it for the first

13

time as he watched the brute come in for the third time, sidling, alert to spring in any direction. But this time, instead of the sidelong flash of the teeth, the dog thrust out his head with only scent to guide it, while his green eyes dwelt constantly on the face of Culver.

The meat was his. He shrank back as he swallowed it, but without shifting his feet. In fact, there appeared to be no danger. Not for an instant was his caution laid aside, but hunger kept him steadily in place until the last morsel of meat was gone. Still the bleeding hand of Culver was held out empty before him. The dog, snarling from the depths of his throat, licked that blood away until the shallow wound was dry.

To Culver, it was an act of infinite grace; for he remembered among primitive people a tasting of blood in the ceremony which creates blood brotherhood. It was a silly fancy, perhaps, that the actions of the dog immediately afterward kept all intimacy at a distance. He returned to his window and sat down before it, oblivious of Culver, oblivious of everything in the world except some undecipherable goal.

It came to Culver, as he reflected, while he cooked his breakfast, that other people in the world had something which differentiated them from him. They had something other than the love of books. They had something beyond images of solemn Etruscans or slant-eyed Orientals. They had deeply possessive love.

He sat down to his bowl of porridge and brown sugar and ate slowly, his eye fixed on the heroic outline of the animal, but his mind groping far beyond the fog that still drifted white against the window. He had a feeling that this dumb brute, like the figurehead of a ship, was traveling over mysterious seas of desire about which he knew nothing. And he wanted to know. There grew up in Culver a blasphemous feeling that he would rather read the mind of the beast than solve the Etruscan mystery.

He put this thought behind him with a guilty haste, washed the porringer, and left the house again, this time to walk a number of blocks until he came to a little corner store which carried notions of all sorts. They had dog muzzles, and he selected a big leather contraption with collar and leash in one. The cost was two dollars and nineteen cents!

And Butcher's edition of the *Poetics,* which by mysterious neglect he had omitted from his library, he could buy from his bookseller for a dollar sixty-three! He broke into a fine sweat as he thought of this. He went home still darkened by this quandary and so pushed open the front door of the house and heard, with horror and fear, the frightful snarling of the dog from the rear of the house. Above that sound rang the screeches of Mrs. Mary Lindley, his landlady, and the sharp, clear voice of a man who spoke with authority. The uproar came from the back yard. He was out on the rear porch instantly. There he saw that his preparations to take the dog for a walk had been much too late; the brute had taken a short cut to exercise and freedom by diving through the window. The ragged remnants of the pane remained, and bright splinters of it were scattered on the cement beneath. On the porch cowered Mrs. Lindley behind a tall young policeman who held a duty revolver in his hand and pointed it down the steps toward the dog.

"Be easy, madam," he was saying. "I'll take care of him if he makes another step toward us."

For down there was that gray monster with his mane ruffed up like a lion's as he advanced a stealthy paw for the next step.

"Put up that gun," said Culver, stepping past the policeman. "I'll handle him. But put that gun out of sight."

"Mr. Culver, Mr. Culver!" wailed the landlady. "What are you after doing to the good name of my house that you bring a wolf into your room? Oh, my God, he'd have the eating of me before he's done. Let me back into the house. Oh, the dirty beast! Officer, Officer, will you do your duty, or will you stand there like a man made of wet dough, and God help us?"

"Put up that gun or I'll take it away from you," said Culver.

"You'll what?" asked the policeman.

Culver held back his hands with a mighty effort.

"Point it another way, then," he said, and walked down the steps straight toward the gray beast that seemed to be stalking them all. Afterward he remembered it all with amazement, wondering at himself, but at the moment he had no earthly fear for himself but only dread that the gun might explode behind him and snuff out the life of the dog. Most wonderful of all, the brute paid not the least attention to him, but allowed the muzzle to be slipped over his head without the slightest attempt to escape. Samuel Culver, fastening it, said to the two at the head of the steps: "You see, he's entirely harmless."

He straightened, smiling at them.

"Harmless?" shrilled Mrs. Lindley. "Harmless, when he's smashed my window to flinders? Oh, Mr. Culver, that you should be playing tricks!"

"Find out if there's a shot of something worth drinking in your house, will you?" asked the policeman; and as Mrs. Lindley disappeared he added to Culver, who was nearing the head of the steps: "What were you saying about taking the gun from me, just now?"

Samuel Culver looked him over with patient calm. He was a big young man, big enough to give trouble and something over; and all the days of his life Culver had prepared

16

his hands for defense merely, never for attack.

"If I've offended you, Officer," said Culver, "I'm very sorry for it."

"Yeah," said the large young policeman. "I've taken a lot of lip from some of you mugs because I was on my beat." He looked at the threadbare clothes, the bagging trousers of Culver, and let his anger run more freely. "But I'm here where there's no one to see," he added, "and it would be only a second for me to peel off this coat and be the same as any man. Why don't you take off your glasses and talk up to me?"

Samuel Culver ran the red tip of his tongue over his lips and narrowed his eyes a little. There is freedom in this world, he thought, for some men to use their hands, and for some dogs to use their teeth, but his own role was that of peace. He said, breathing a little hard as he spoke the words: "I want no trouble with you, sir!"

"Ah, that's it, is it?" murmured the man of the law. He sneered openly. "It's only the clothes you wear that are big, eh?" And he turned away with a shrug of his fine shoulders. Culver walked slowly past him. The dog followed without pulling back on the leash, but snarling savagely at every step. So they came back into the room.

CHAPTER 4

It was not the same room that it had been for nine years before. In place of the fine old musty odor of the books there was a taint of sea in the moist air. It was not as though a mere pane had been knocked out of a window; it was as

17

though a whole wall were down, letting the raw San Francisco air come billowing in, blowing its visible breath into every corner. In a strange way, it seemed to Samuel Culver as though waves of the sea were washing over his books, over his aspirations, and leaving only a soggy ruin behind.

He tied the dog to a leg of the bed and sat down on it to put his thoughts in order before he began his day's work; but every moment he remained there the work became more and more distasteful to him. He decided to take the dog for a walk.

The leash made all the difference. It exercised a miraculous control, and the big dog never let the strap grow taut. To see this wild spirit so thoroughly controlled was like watching a bushman do a toe-dance. Yet when they reached the street, Culver was not leading him; he was leading Culver. For he walked out to the end of the lead, keeping his head slightly turned like some small boy beckoning another forward. Culver obediently followed to the corner from which he had first seen the dog galloping through the mist, then out into the street, where the big fellow went in an eager zigzag with his nose close to the pavement. When the traffic flowed down the street to the south, he jumped to the sidewalk, but returned to his study the moment the pavement was safe.

Whatever sign he sought for, Culver knew that oil and water drippings and the rub of ten thousand tires had wiped it out long ago, but he was touched by the persistence of the dog. So a good scholar patiently goes over and over the page in search of the little things which may lead into great answers.

Suddenly the dog stood back on the sidewalk with his head raised, pointing into the wind, and his eyes almost closed. What did the wind tell that sensitive organism, of tarry odors from the wharves, and cookery in a thousand

18

kitchens?

Then, determined on a new course of action, or else finding something in the wind that served as a clue, he turned suddenly about and led off, his head still half-turned as though imploring Culver to follow. And Culver followed—almost reverently—the passion of this animal in the search. He saw that he was being taken down toward the water front, with its rumblings of trucks and hootings of whistles that kept the sky busy with noise. Now they were turning up a side street. The dog veered, and started up a flight of steps over which hung the sign: ROOMS: BY THE MONTH AND TRANSIENT.

At the very end of the leash he paused while Culver made up his mind; then Culver followed and rang the bell. The door was opened by a bald little man with a bright nose, like a red dab of paint in the middle of his face.

"No dogs," he said. "Can't keep dogs—get that brute out of here!" For the gray dog had entered the dark hallway past the proprietor.

"Certainly," agreed Culver. "But are you sure that the master of this fellow hasn't been here?"

"Not with him. Not that I know of," came the answer. "Trot right along with him, brother."

Culver fumbled in his pocket and brought out a fifty-cent piece.

"Suppose you let him walk in—and right out again?" he pleaded. "He seems to be going somewhere."

The proprietor took the money, spun it in the air, let it spat against the palm of his hand. The solid thump of the half dollar against his skin seemed to decide him.

"All right," he said. "But step lively. Lay him alow or aloft, and get him out again. I can't have a dog messing up a decent place."

Culver followed the dog into the hallway. Straight up-

19

stairs he was led, past a weather-stained print of an old clipper that flew through a storm under upper topsails only, with the bone in her teeth. With a perfect surety the dog was clambering on, turning left in the upper hall. Now he paused in the dimness at a closed door and sniffed the crack at the bottom of it. Culver tapped gently. Voices ceased in the room.

"Who's there?" barked a man.

"I wanted to know if a dog—" began Culver.

The door jerked open. A man as squat and bowlegged as a bulldog stood in trousers and undershirt on the threshold. On one arm a golden nymph rode a purple dolphin. On the other the Stars and Stripes waved from elbow to shoulder above a pair of battling seagulls on the lower arm.

"Hey! Lookat!" called the husky voice of a woman. "Lookat, Jack! That ain't a dog. It's a plush horse!"

She lolled back in an armchair with the fat of her legs crossed. The make-up that had made her young the night before had smudged crookedly and gave her a lopsided face. She had a half-glass of beer in her hand, and the liquid sloshed up nearly to the brim as she shook with laughter.

"The dog is looking for something," said Culver, "and he wants to try to find it in this room. Will you tell me if you ever have seen him before?"

The sailor leaned to stare. A snarl, a flash of teeth that made the muzzle seem more fragile than tissue paper, sent him backward a stumbling pace or two.

"Maybe I've seen him, but he's never seen me," said the sailor.

"Come here, honey. Come here and see Aunt Molly," said the woman, smiling and turning coy for the dog. "Babies and dogs, they always come to me. If I had my rights, I'd have a house full of them. Come here, sweetheart, and see Aunt Molly. . . . Oh, go to hell, then, you ugly beast! Get

20

him out of here, Jack. Throw 'em out, if you're a man!"

For the dog, sniffing rapidly across the rug, had paid her no attention.

"Move on," said Jack, waving his thick arm toward the door. "We've had enough of you both. Take your dunnage and roll ashore, will you?"

"One moment!" pleaded Culver, as the dog scratched back the edge of the rug and tried vainly to pick up some small object with his teeth. Culver picked up from the floor a little ebony cross bound with silver rope at the crossing. The dog leaped for it, almost knocking it out of his grasp with the thrust of his nose. Culver put it in his pocket.

"What's he got?" asked Molly. "Take it away from him, Jack."

"No," said Jack, sea-law asserting itself in his moral mind. "No: finders, keepers. Barge along, brother."

"Will you tell me when you took this room?" asked Culver, passing back into the hall.

"Last night. This morning, I mean—and what the hell is it to you?" asked Jack.

He slammed the door, and Culver went slowly down the stairs. He was no longer led by his companion. The dog followed at his side, frantically nuzzling his coat pocket, and making deep in his throat that whining noise which was hardly distinguishable from a snarl except that there was added to the sound an almost human note of inquiry.

The proprietor was waiting impatiently at the front door.

"You've taken long enough," he said. "Good-by to you and your dog—and what kind of a shenanigan is this, anyway?"

"Someone he knows has been here," answered Samuel Culver. "Will you tell me who had that room last night, or yesterday? The third door to the left from the head of the stairs."

21

"What you want to know about him?" asked the proprietor. "I dunno who you're talking about, anyway."

"I think he's the master of this dog," insisted Culver.

"Ah, damn the dog!" said the old man, and pushed Culver through the door.

He stood for a moment on the porch, adding up, while the dog kept nuzzling the pocket which held the treasure. What human picture came to him with the scent of the cross, Culver would have given much to know; but all he could tell was that he had found a lodestone to which the dog now pointed, as though a powerful magnet had been placed near a compass and drawn it from its true north.

The whole sidewalk for the moment was clotted with a heavy traffic, and into the thick of it the dog pushed himself with return of the old eagerness of the trail. Culver, surprised and pleased, followed the leash once more until he identified the subject of this new quest. It was a stocky man with red hair that bristled out beneath his hat, and a fire-red neck; a thick-set, powerful man of thirty or more, who walked with a sailor's swaggering step.

They had come almost to this stranger when a change of the traffic lights cut off the crowd. The dog's quarry crossed the street in a hurry as the east-west traffic began to flow, leaving Culver impatiently on the edge of the curb. That impatience grew as he saw his man enter a taxi. All he gained was a glimpse of the profile, a stubbed and blunted profile with apelike brows that jutted out almost as much as the nose. The taxi carried him away, while the dog, without putting the least tension on the leash, reared and whined in his desire to follow.

There was only one way to follow now, and luck brought an empty cab past them at this moment. Culver stopped it with a wave of his hand.

"That cab down there in the next block—follow it—follow it fast. Catch up with it, will you? I've got to speak to that man."

He had the dog inside. They started on the jump as he slammed the door and sat forward on the edge of his seat. The gray dog watched also, hanging his head out the window and pointing forward anxiously. The pursuit kept weaving toward the north until they started up the sharp slope of Telegraph Hill. Then the inevitable happened. A change of lights cut them off at the next corner. Culver groaned till he saw the cab that led them actually pulling up to the curb in full view. It had paused in front of a small house with a splash of green garden running down to the sidewalk. It was a white house, and there was a girl in white in front of it with the sun glistening on her dress; and the sun made a red jewel out of her hair, as she chatted with the man who had stepped from the cab. The traffic light fortunately changed as the stocky fellow turned back to his taxi, but unfortunately a truck had forged ahead too far, and a traffic officer appeared from nowhere to deliver a lecture, together with a ticket. He halted everything in the meantime; before he stepped back and waved the automobiles on their way, all hope was gone from poor Culver. He stopped the car and paid his fare on the far side of the street. Once more the price of Butcher's *Poetics* had disappeared from his pocket; he felt it like the loss of blood.

There remained nothing before him that offered even the shadow of a clue except the girl in the white dress. He headed for her with the dog at his side, pointing again continually at the pocket in which the ebony cross was hidden.

CHAPTER 5

The fog had broken up, and the sun was making white crystal of the girl's dress as she leaned with a trowel to work at her garden. When Culver came to the edge of the lawn, he took off his hat and waited. The dog sat down with his muzzle pressed against the pocket which held the treasure. How to begin such a conversation as this, Culver had very little idea, so he stood waiting until the girl looked up.

"Do you want something?" she asked.

"I can't say that I do, or that I have a right—" said Culver, and halted, finding that words came with difficulty.

"Should I know you?" she asked. "I'm no good at re-membering faces. Or do you know me? What a magnificent dog! What a glorious dog!"

She held out her hand toward him; though his back was turned, he seemed to sense the gesture, and that soul-stopping snarl came out of his throat as he whirled about.

"Steady, boy," cautioned Culver. "I'm sorry," he apologized.

"That doesn't matter," said the girl. "You can't ask pretty manners out of a thunderbolt, can you? What's his name?"

"I don't know," said Culver.

"Hi, Sally!" called a voice from the open house door. "Hi! I've got it!"

He was a streamlined young man of at least a 1940 model. The sweeping way in which he brushed his hair, the easy room which his legs found in his trousers without dis-turbing their pressed edge, and the sea-brown color of his face were all even more than up to date.

"I've got it, old girl!" he called again. "Right on the nose! Come on in and hear Australia."

"Coming in a minute, Tommy," answered Sally, and turned back to Culver with the smile for Tommy still shining in her eyes.

" 'Not for the words but for the manner of them,' " quoted Culver. " 'Not for the face, but something shining through it.' A very handsome young man. A brother, perhaps—or a husband?"

"Not a brother," said Sally. "And not quite a husband."

"I hope the good day will come soon," answered Culver. "How frank you are! How charmingly frank and open! Hidden thoughts leave a shadow on the face, as someone says, somewhere. Was it beautiful old Firdusi?"

"Who was he?" asked the girl.

"He was one of the modern Persian poets. Well, not exactly modern, but not so many centuries ago. But Tommy has something to show you, and I must not keep you here."

The girl smiled and was turning to go when something stopped her to say: "But wasn't there something you wanted to know, at first?"

"Was there?" echoed Culver, rather at sea, for it was easy for him to grow absent-minded at the slightest provocation. "Ah, but of course there was: I wanted to ask about the man who was in the taxicab, the one who spoke to you."

"Do you know him?" she asked.

"I don't," said Culver. "But I've an idea that he is the master of this dog. I picked him up, straying, the other day, and his heart is breaking to get home."

"But he's devoted to you. He won't leave you for an instant!"

"I have a relic of his master in my pocket. That's why he stays so close," answered Culver, sighing. "There's a spe-

25

cial beauty about that, don't you think? A devotion so perfect that even a trinket is loved because the master has touched it?"

It seemed to Culver that something about these words drew the girl so that she came a little closer to him.

"I'd like to know you," she said.

"Would you?" asked Culver, astonished. "You would like to know me? But you may, of course, as much as you please. That is to say, when I've found the dog's master, and then a job."

"Are you out of work?" she asked, puckering her forehead.

"Oh, I'll find something presently," said Culver. "But I'm keeping you from Tommy still. If you only could tell me where I can find the man who was just talking to you—"

"I haven't the slightest idea," she answered. "He wanted to know if I could locate another man for him. Walter Toth, an uncle of mine that I haven't seen or heard of for a dozen years. He wanted to know if I could give him an idea where Walter Toth might be—somewhere in the South Seas; and I hadn't the foggiest notion. So he left—like that. I never saw him before."

"What a pity!" murmured Culver.

"Look!" said the girl. "Come in a moment and talk to Tommy. His father is putting men to work all the time. Lumber. It wouldn't be much of a job, but it might be a stopgap. Do come in."

"Won't I disturb you?" asked Culver.

But she had him by the arm, drawing him forward in spite of the tremendous snarling of the dog. Culver, bewildered by this cordiality, tied the dog to the handrail by the steps, and went inside with her. It was a double house, with the girl's family living in one side of it and Tommy on the other.

26

Thomas Wiley was standing back from his work and wiping his hands.

"It's going to knock them over, Sally," he said. "They'll have to put that on every good radio in the world, I think; and when the cash begins to come in—"

He looked steadily at her. The girl flushed with happiness, but she touched Culver with a brief gesture. "Mr. Culver's out of work," she said. "Tommy, your father can help him, somehow."

"If you say so, he can and will," answered Tommy. "Will you tell me what you can do, Mr. Culver?"

"I could do translation," said Culver.

"What languages?" asked Tommy.

"The Romance tongues, of course," said Culver, "and the Scandinavian and German and Dutch, also Russian and Chinese; my Japanese is quite imperfect, I'm sorry to say. And in Arabic I'm a little out of touch. I'm sorry about that, too."

"In lumber!" exclaimed the girl.

This singular remark caused Tommy to wince a little. "But lumber is the old man's job, after all," he said. "Mr. Culver, could you keep books?"

"What a pity!" sighed Culver. "My own accounts never will tally correctly. So I'm quite sure that I couldn't keep books."

"Have you ever done any selling? Canvassing? Anything like that?"

"I'm sorry that I've had no experience," apologized Culver. "But if there were a place in the business requiring manual labor, that would be an advantage to me."

"Ah?" said the girl, with a strange irony in her voice. "Have you done manual labor?"

"No. I've worked in an express office as a writer of labels, you understand. But I think manual labor would be better.

It would pay as much, and it would leave me without the necessity of taking exercise."

"Yes. It would do that," said Sally, looking sternly at Tommy. "It would save that time for you. Now, Mr. Culver, Tommy is going to think of something. Will you come to dinner?"

"To dinner?" asked Culver, amazed. "But I never go out!"

"I want you to come. Come for dinner, please," she said. "In my house just next door. . . . Romance languages—that means you know French and Spanish and Italian, I suppose?"

"Oh, yes," said Culver. "You take all three in a breath, don't you think? They're so thoroughly rooted in Latin."

"In a breath?" repeated the girl. "Well, will you come to dinner—tonight?"

"How very kind of you!" said Samuel Culver. He went toward the door.

"At seven-thirty," said the girl. "Tommy will have thought of something."

"I shall be here," said Culver. "It's odd," he murmured as he paused in the doorway. "I feel as though the burdens had been taken away." He looked into the girl's face without seeing her features. "I think I understand now," said Culver, "what the poets mean by the touch of ultimate grace."

He left the house on Telegraph Hill in a pleasant haze so unusual that he almost forgot the dog walking beside him as he swung along on the way toward home. When an explanation came to him, the shock of it stopped him stock-still on a corner curb.

Pity! It might be pity that had stirred her. Suddenly he wished to be alone with his books, immersed in the uncounted centuries of them, walled in by their eloquence and

28

their wisdom; for only the dead speak words that are not barbed with poison.

Someone said: "Heads up, fellow!"

That was the tall young policeman who had come to the rescue of Mrs. Lindley.

Culver halted.

"The next time you walk that dog out with no license, I'm going to take and jam him in the pound, and they'll give him a whiff of gas," said the policeman. He gave Culver a sneer, and walked on. And as he walked, he laughed.

He laughed, and Tommy had smiled. From the very beginning it had been like that for Samuel Pennington Culver. His schoolmates, in the old days, had laughed in his face, or smiled. There were always the poverty-stricken clothes, and that earnest, patient, plodding manner. It was as though the rest of the world possessed some superior knowledge of life and the ways of society which for his part he lacked. Perhaps it was that sense of difference which had caused him to make his isolation more perfect and shelter himself in the world of his books.

Culver reached the rooming house. As he pushed open the front door, the shrill voice of Mrs. Lindley came down the stairs.

"Culver?" she asked.

"Yes," he called back.

"Have you got that filthy brute of a dog with you?"

"I have the dog," he admitted.

"Well, you'll have to get him out," she shouted. "I won't have him around the place. This ain't a kennel. And there's six dollars and fifty cents for the glazier for fixing the broken window. I'll thank you to have that ready for me in the morning!"

When he got in the room, he removed the muzzle of the dog. He was thirsty, which reminded him that the dog might be, also, so he filled a basin with water and put it on the floor. The big fellow stood over it and wolfed it up with a passionate need. And somehow the ache went out of Culver's heart, for a moment.

But how could he avoid returning to the white house? That was the problem which troubled him most. He looked anxiously toward the bright new pane in the window. Six dollars and fifty cents!

He dared not give the animal the freedom of the room if window-smashing was the order of the day, so he tied the leash to the leg of the bed and went to his books. But they were no good. Nothing would stay in his mind.

Something had to be done about the white house. He went to the hall telephone. He found the number of a Thomas Wiley on Telegraph Hill and called it. That clear young voice, easily recognizable, returned to him over the wire.

"Mr. Wiley," said Culver, "I regret that I cannot come this evening for dinner. Will you tell the lady? The fact is that I can't leave my dog in my room without having him break up things; and if I take him into the street, I'll be arrested for having no license for him."

"He can't come," translated the voice of Wiley, full of an obvious relief. "Dog won't let him go. . . ." Then he added: "Wait a moment. Sally wants to speak to you."

"This is Sally Franklin," she was saying. "Mr. Culver, are you sure that you can't break away? I've been counting on seeing you again."

"It would be pleasant," answered Culver, tasting and retasting the sound of her voice. "But unless you could come here, I don't see how—and of course you and Mr. Wiley wouldn't want to—"

"Come there for dinner? Of course we'd come there!" cried the girl.

A dim roar of protest sounded in the distance.

30

"Tommy couldn't make it, but I'll make it. May I come?" she was asking.

Another roar of protest issued from the background. With dismay, Culver thought of his room, heaped and crowded with books. But what could he say? He found himself giving his address. Seven o'clock would be the hour for the meal. He was not to make any special preparations. She would have exactly what he had intended for himself.

"Rice?" he thought. Would she have been contented with rice—and apples bought at a third the usual rate because they were unsound and had to have the spots of dry rot cut out of their cheeks?

No, he would have to get something else for her. . . . This brought him again to the money question. From his remaining store he counted out the six dollars and fifty cents which was the cost of the windowpane, and discovered with a stone-cold heart that there remained to him exactly fifteen cents in silver and three in copper. He looked wildly around his room. In the entire world he had nothing worth a price with the exception of his books. The thought shocked him as a blasphemy would have shocked the high priest of a temple. Yet he picked up a whole armful of his treasures, jammed a hat on his head, and went out, with a feeling that the deluge was upon him.

He went to Farbenstein's, first.

"Mr. Farbenstein," said Samuel Culver, "I have to cook a meal for a lady. Will you kindly tell me what I should give her?"

"A lady? You cook a meal for a lady?" echoed Farbenstein. "Young or old?"

"Young, if you please," said Culver.

"Young, eh?" snapped Farbenstein. "Then it looks as though it was your pleasure, not mine, Mr. Culver. For a young lady, make it steak. Young ladies once ate chicken wings, and didn't cost much. But young ladies today ride horses and hit golf balls and swim and play tennis, and they eat steak—rare. A good tenderloin, or a fine sirloin at fifty-five cents a pound; and baking potatoes; and a head of lettuce; and oil and vinegar and English mustard for a dressing; and best coffee; and maybe a grapefruit to begin, and ice cream for ending it. If eating is the end, eh?"

He leered at Culver.

"I'll be back," said Culver, sickened by the face of the man, and by the thought of this mountainous expense. "How much for everything?"

"Why, maybe two dollars and a half would almost cover everything," answered Farbenstein.

Two dollars and a half! Culver could live for eight days on such a sum; but perhaps it was fine food that gave to Sally Franklin the aroma and the delicacy of beauty in spite of her deviation from the classical canon. Perhaps it was the abandon of gay good living that enabled other people to smile down at Culver's vegetarian existence?

Reaching the shop of James McPherson, he paused at the entrance of the cellar store to inhale for a moment that musty fragrance which roused in his imagination a chorus of dim, great voices from the past.

"Ah-ha!" called a rusty voice.

There was James McPherson, nodding and smiling. He was a pale old man with skin almost as white as his hair. "Here is the Butcher. I knew you'd be back for it. I knew you'd be back!"

Culver, descending, said: "This time I've come to sell, not to buy."

"To sell? To sell?" said McPherson, losing his smile. "What's happened to you, Mr. Culver? Not whisky? Not women, I hope?"

He teetered forward a little, staring at the glasses of

32

Culver, trying to penetrate his mind. The mere mention of women, it was plain, roused up the evil in every man!

"Well," said McPherson, "what have you brought me?"

"I don't know," answered Culver, and put the pile of books on a table.

"You don't know, eh?" gasped McPherson. "Are you daft, man? Bringing me books that you don't know?"

"Ah, I know them well enough," said Culver, identifying them with one sweeping glance. His heart seemed to go out of him with his breath, as he spoke. "It's the Spinoza that I can do best without, because I have two other sets of him. I can do without the Spinoza. But not the Lucian. It's Gluckman's Lucian, and I can't do without that!"

He reached out anxious hands toward the volumes. If he were leaving his Lucian, was he not leaving all tiptoe gayety and charming frivolity out of his life? What is Voltaire but a handful of thumbs compared with the exquisite touch of Lucian?

"Not Lucian!" repeated Culver. "But what will you give me for the Spinoza? I paid you more than three dollars for the set."

"You paid!" snarled McPherson. "You paid for a fine, crisp set, clean and clear. But see this stain, and look at that rumpled edge. These books are worth nothing to me. No, I'll remember that you're an old customer. For your sake, not for the sake of the books, I'll give you a dollar on them!"

The big man took off his glasses, wiped them clean, and then settled them back on his nose again.

"Only one dollar for Spinoza!" he said. "But if a man were to go to a desert island, with only one case of books to keep him company forever, he would have to have his Spinoza along. As surely as Christ died for the world, Spinoza lived and thought for it. Well, there is nothing I can do about it! But women, women—Mr. McPherson, women are a deadly sweet poison in the air, are they not?"

"So it is a woman, is it?" asked McPherson. He laughed a little. "Take an old man's advice. Throw her off. Away with her. At your age, she doesn't love you for your face; and when did a woman ever love a man for his mind? And when did—"

The steady, coldly critical eye with which he found Culver watching him stopped the tongue of McPherson.

"Look at the Lucian, then," said Culver. "The Gluck-man notes are the best."

He said it shortly and turned half away. He wanted to be out of this place; the shadow of it fell upon his soul like a contagion upon the body.

"Well, this is a little better," said McPherson. "A little better, but not much. These are finger-worn books, Mr. Culver. However, I could offer you, say, a dollar and a half?"

The shock passed right through the brain of Culver, like an arrowpoint.

"A dollar and a half!" he whispered. But the matter was clinched in his mind by the realization that his armful of books would bring in exactly the money he needed to buy food for Sally Franklin. . . . The very name, by this time, was poison in his thoughts.

CHAPTER 6

He thought that he had allowed plenty of time. As a matter of fact, he was bending over the fumes of the steak when Sally Franklin came. When he brought her in, the mist from the frying-pan was thick across his glasses, so that she was hardly more than a blur.

Farbenstein had told him how to prepare everything. He had laid out the table, he had taken for himself the blue plate with the chip out of one side, and given to the girl the pink plate covered with tumbling designs of roses. Women like such gay things, of course. He lacked anything but a tin cup, but he had a good uncracked saucer to put under it. He had given her the knife to which some of the silver plating still adhered; and from the center of the table he had cleared away the stacks of books, so that there would be room for her. He did not mind sitting a bit sidewise, himself.

One organ-deep growl from the dog greeted the entrance of the girl. After that, he returned to his contemplation of the window and that desired mystery of the outer night, oblivious of the human beings in the room. His dignity was impeccable.

A nervous concern about the beefsteak overwhelmed the mind of Culver. He glanced at his watch. The steak had been on for eleven minutes, casting up clouds of smoke.

"Beefsteak," he said. "The butcher tells me that girls like beefsteak, in these days. It is true?"

"I like it," said Sally.

"Rare?" he inquired, the iron fork poised anxiously.

"Medium," she told him.

"Ah, he was wrong, then. He said that young women liked rare meat," observed Culver. "Then in three more minutes—will you try the salad dressing? Is it too oily?"

"It is perfect," she answered, dipping a twist of lettuce into the bowl and tasting it.

He carried the steak, still spitting and steaming in the pan, to the table and transferred it to her plate. In haste he poured over it the juice from the pan. The steak quite filled the plate. Jumping in haste to the stove again, he snatched a pair of potatoes from the oven. He laid them on the table beside her steak. The butter he pushed nearer. The salad dressing he poured over the lettuce in the tin bowl. The coffee, next; adhering strictly to the letter of Farbenstein's instructions, he ran some cold water down the spout and then poured forth a stream of the liquid into the tin cup.

"There is also ice cream for you," said Culver, beginning to relax.

"Aren't you carving this steak in two? Where's your share?" she asked, staring at his empty plate.

He poured a stream of white rice onto the plate and shook his head.

"This is my supper," he said. "Meat? I haven't tasted it in years and years. If you think of the people who lived almost entirely without it, you'll see that I've taken a healthy diet. And this cauliflower gives bulk and vitamins. . . . Is everything all right?"

"Everything is perfect," she answered, looking not at the food but directly at him. "Except that I can't eat half of this."

"Can't you?" asked Culver, surprised. "Don't you ride and swim and play tennis and golf?"

"Now and then," she admitted.

"But then you eat large quantities of meat, don't you?" inquired Culver.

"Did the butcher tell you these things?" she wanted to know.

"He did," agreed Culver.

"What a clever butcher he turned out to be," said the girl. And she began to laugh.

Culver took a good mouthful of rice and smiled and nodded at her.

36

"Very pleasant! How very pleasant!" he said. "Don't stop, please!"

"What do you mean?" she asked.

"The laughter," said Culver. "It lifts your chin and gives your throat a lovely line. And though your mouth is a little crooked, I hardly notice it; and I forget the highness of your cheekbones, too; and all at once you are shining so that I see only the brightness, as though you were made only of color in a light."

She looked at him with startled eyes.

Culver drew out a notebook. "I must make a record," he stated, "if you will pardon me. I must keep the observation that beauty is perhaps essentially bright. So darkness suggests the unknown, and the unknown is what we fear; but light suggests knowledge, and knowledge is beauty, and beauty knowledge. Keats, of course, said it in different words. You permit me to make the note?"

The startled look was quite gone from her eyes. Instead, they crinkled a bit at the corners as she watched him.

"Of course I permit you," she said. "And I suppose," she added, "that my mouth is crooked."

"It is," agreed Culver, who knew nothing except to speak the truth. "It's singular, isn't it, that although my eye tells me that you are far from the Phidian canon, a spirit inside me keeps telling my heart that you are perfectly lovely."

"This is very strange, of course," said the girl, and she looked him straight in the eye with a certain sternness.

"But obviously you are unlike other people, as Sappho was unlike other poets. They speak; she sings. You remember the lines—"

"I don't read Greek," she said.

"Not really!" cried Culver. "I would have said that you were all Greek. How many people have laughed at me, and always given me pain. But your laughter was a delight."

37

"Was it?" she said, and laughed again.

He was enchanted. "Continue! Encore! Encore!" he cried.

"But I can't laugh forever," she said, laughing still.

"If you could see yourself," said Culver, "you never would stop. You are touched by a miracle, when you laugh. It is something which I never could put in my notebook. This is how Euphrosyne laughed, and all the Olympians could not keep themselves from happiness. Oh, Homer, now I understand!"

"What is it you understand?" asked the girl.

"What the old men thought to themselves as they sat on the walls of Troy," answered Culver. "But you are eating nothing. And it is growing cold."

"How can I eat, when you talk to me like this?" she wanted to know. "Do you often talk as you've been talking to me?"

"No, never," said Culver, anxiously. "Because I never talk with women."

"You will, however," she stated.

"I don't think so," he told her.

"Oh, but you will, and you mustn't," she said.

"I won't, then," agreed Culver humbly. "Will you tell me what I said that was wrong?"

"I can't tell you," she answered, shaking her head. "It's something that you simply have to know."

"I want to learn. Perhaps from you," said Culver, "I can learn why people always have smiled at me, and laughed behind my back. But you, laughing to my face, have been only delightful."

"If people have smiled at you," she said, "it's because your eyes have been too high to watch where your feet were stumbling."

"That is something I shall have to consider before I understand it," said Culver, attentive as a pupil in a class.

. . . "Have you eaten all you can?"

"And everything was delicious," she said. "I've never had such a good time. Why does your face fall when I say that?"

"As Goethe says—and sometimes he was both good and wise: 'One sees the intention and becomes depressed.' So I see your intention of kindness, and I am a little depressed. Forgive me. I know there has been nothing here but poor food, and bad service, and a crowded room—"

He looked around him and it seemed to him that he was seeing his room for the first time.

"I have brought you into a kennel!" said Culver. "And I have given you nothing but cold food, and talk!"

"But such talk!"

"It offended you!"

"Offended? It will never be out of my ears. It will ring and ring in my ears. I'll never be really unhappy again. I've only to remember what you've said about me, and then I'll have to appreciate my own company. It was hardly talk at all."

"You have made me feel rich," he said. "You have taken all the trouble away. Like Hope. You know the fable."

"Of Pandora? Thank God, I do!"

"Why do you say it in such a way?" he asked.

"Because I am thankful to know one thing that you refer to!"

"Ah, I refer to books—I am too bookish, and sometimes people don't quite understand. I shall make a note of that and try to be better," said he.

"If you change yourself in one slightest way, I'll never forgive you," said the girl. "But the world will change you soon enough, probably—in spite of these fences and walls of books that you've built around yourself. . . . Speaking of that, here is a note that Tommy sent for you. You are to

39

take it to his father's office. And now—it is ten; but I wish I could stay for hours and hours more."

"If you wish that, it is almost the same as though you had stayed," said Culver. "And it gives me permission to imagine you still in the room until midnight and after—which will be very companionable and pleasant."

She looked at the floor, at the books, and then at Culver. She said nothing at all. The silence endured for an alarming moment until he said: "Is that something which I should not have told you?"

Still she considered for an instant before she said: "No. I think you can say anything to me. But only to me."

"Because other people would not understand?" he questioned.

"That's exactly it. They wouldn't understand," replied the girl.

He went out with her to the front porch. He walked down the steps with her to the street. It was a clear night.

"See how clean the sky is!" said Culver, as he took her to her car. "As though the fog had been used to wash it this morning."

"Do you need those huge lenses in order to see?" she asked.

"I'm afraid I do," he said.

"Will you take them off for a moment?"

"Certainly," he agreed, and removed them from his nose.

"Can you see me now?"

"Yes, I can see you. But it's rather a misty picture."

"Are you going to work yourself quite blind?" she asked.

"Don't pity me, please," urged Culver. "I have a wonderfully happy life, in fact. That is, I've always thought it was happy. . . . But don't pity me, will you?"

He could see her, rather vaguely, lift her hand to her lips, and then the fingertips touched his eyes quickly and

40

lightly. It surprised Culver so much that he had not even wits to say good night, as she slipped into the car and drove away.

CHAPTER 7

Culver returned to his room and forced his hands to obey him until the dishes were washed. There was a great deal of the meat left. He cut it small and fed it to the dog. It was wolfed down greedily, and his hand was licked clean afterward.

It was easy to advance to this stage of familiarity with the huge beast; but not a step farther—the moment the feeding obviously was ended, the big dog turned away his head, truly like a nobleman from his gutter-bred servant. It came over Culver that he could serve the beast for a thousand years and be no nearer to him than poor Egyptian peasants were to Anubis, the divine jackal.

When he stood up and looked about him, it was extraordinary how small and wretched the room appeared. A singular unrest possessed him, body and soul, and he determined to take the dog for a night excursion.

So he muzzled the big dog and took him on the leash down to the street. At once he found himself being led—heading down for the water front again. There was no turning up side streets on this occasion. Instead, the dog took him across the big open thoroughfare in front of the piers and led him close to the piers for block after block. He turned to the right, at last, to a pier-side where a three-masted sailing ship was tethered by ropes that looked inadequate to the work. There was enough stir in the hull to keep the mastheads swinging slightly across the stars.

The dog became more and more excited as he drew near the gangplank. Culver had small chance to take special note of the craft, except that the bow was extraordinarily fine.

"Yeah, and who are you, buddy?" asked a man from the waist of the ship, standing up out of the shadows.

"The dog," said Culver, "seems to know this vessel. And I had an idea that perhaps someone here might tell me the name of his master."

"Wait a minute," said the sailor.

He walked aft to the break of the poop and sang out: "Hi, Mister!"

A voice roared an indistinct answer.

"There's a mug here with Napico," said the sailor.

Footfalls sounded aft. A man came out and stood looming big against the sky.

"You're batty, Joe," he said.

"Take a look for yourself down there in the gangplank," answered Joe.

"Mister" hurried down the ladder to the deck and was instantly at the gangplank.

"Yeah. It's him," he said. "By God, it is him. Leave go the line, stranger, and let him come aboard."

"Certainly," said Culver; but as he saw that alert figure of the dog and felt the tremor coming up the tautness of the line, his heart was pinched small. If he let the leash go, the dog would be gone with it, forever; and presently a whole ocean would lie between him and this strange event. For the dog, he felt, had been like an opening door which had admitted him already into a new existence, and the promise of things still more strange. It was due to the dog that he had been led to Sally Franklin, for instance, and her name was no longer a poison in the air he breathed.

42

"I wonder," said Culver, "if I could find the master of the dog on board?"

"Sure. He belongs here, don't he?" asked Mister. "If you can see anything, you can see that!"

"But his master?" asked Culver.

"I'm his master," said Mister. "Come along like a good fellow, Pico."

The dog answered first with a shuddering vibration that Culver felt distinctly up the strap, and then with a growl of murderous hatred.

"Why, damn you!" said Mister. "Why, damn you, I've got a mind to brain you, you—"

"Look, Mister," said Joe, "what good is that cutthroat to us now? Who wants him aboard, anyway? Who ever would want him, except—"

"Shut that crazy mouth of yours, will you?" commanded Mister. "I didn't hear your name, sir?"

"Because I didn't speak it," said Culver, with his customary frankness. "But my name is Samuel Culver."

"I knew a Sam Cutler in New Orleans, one voyage," said Mister. "He was a fine hand with the cards, and at dice he was no slouch, either. Why don't you come on board for a minute or two, and the skipper will be along."

"I thought you said that you were the owner of the dog?" asked Culver.

"Why, I'm the mate of the *Spindrift*," answered Mister. "I'm Jerry Burke, and when the Old Man's below, I'm on deck in his name over everything in the ship. I stand in his place most of the time, d'you see, and that's why I said that I was the brute's master. Though God knows, there's only one master for him in the world. Come aboard for a yarn, Mr. Cutler, and the skipper will be along in no time at all."

Culver went aboard. There was a certain unwillingness to his feet, and a weakness in his knees of which he was aware; and he knew that a voice was calling him a fool, for there was something smugly sinister about Jerry Burke; the ship's lantern showed him smiling and extending a welcome with his waving hand, and yet there was a sneer behind his smiling, as though he despised the fool who trusted his words and could not keep his contempt from showing its teeth.

Yet Culver's feet took him up the gangplank. He saw a strip as of metal between the wharf and the side of the *Spindrift.* That was the water of the bay gleaming faintly. Crossing that, he entered that other and outer world of the sea, with its new language and new laws. He stepped down on the deck and at once felt beneath his feet the slight motion, the liquid sway and yielding of the ship as it wavered beside the pier, as though even in harbor she still felt the danger of the sea.

He looked up to the wide-spreading yards, then down to the slender hull, and wondered. Even in her sleep she stirred beside the pier with dreams of the ocean.

"Now what you think of our giblet pie?" asked the mate, following Culver's glance.

"Giblet pie?" echoed Culver.

"I mean," said Mister, "that the *Spindrift* is all wings and legs. She's been a flyer, brother. She's had her Melbourne days, her China days, and she's been blackbirding, too."

"*Spindrift—Spindrift—*" murmured Culver. "I think that I've heard of the name."

The dog was at the far end of the leash, still trembling, and facing right aft, forgetting even to snarl at Mister.

"You think you've heard the name," echoed the mate. "Maybe you've heard of *Cutty Sark* and *Thermopylae,* and God Almighty too! But the fact is that this isn't the great *Spindrift* that wore the big main course, the biggest mains'l

44

in the China Sea. This is a sort of a stepdaughter of that old girl, as you might say."

"Extremely interesting," said Culver; "but since the skipper is not here, I'd better go back. I'll leave my name and address, if he wants to come for the dog."

"Why, but he'll be back in a minute," said Burke. "I'll hold the dog, if you want."

He looked past Culver and made a motion with his head. Culver felt rather than saw the other sailor step behind him. All the logic of his mind told him that there could be no danger. But all the instinct in him was crying out.

"I'd better keep the dog till I'm sure," said Culver.

"Till you're sure?" shouted Burke in a sudden rage. "Can't you see that the dog's at home?"

There was a good deal of truth in that, of course; but Culver answered: "It seems to me that this dog isn't at home either on a ship or on shore, anywhere, until he finds his master. That's what I'm interested in. Not the places he's familiar with, but the man who owns him. . . . Have you anybody on board," he added, "who dares to take the muzzle off that dog?"

There was a bit of a silence. Culver felt more assured than ever.

"If there's anybody on the ship," he said, "who has the courage to do that, I'll leave the dog on board."

"Or else?" asked Burke.

"Or else, I'll have to take him back."

"All right, Joe," said Mister.

Something stirred behind Culver. He whirled about and stepped back from the shadow of the coming blow. He saw the face of Joe twisted up so that the eyes became almost invisible; but his teeth were grinning as his lips stretched back in a wide contortion of the mouth. He had had to work up his resolution quickly for this act. He was not

45

striking straight out. It was a down-pawing motion. There was enough of the boxer in Culver to block the striking hand, but something whipped over his raised arm. . . . The leather-covered blackjack struck him squarely between the eyes and dropped him into a thousand miles of darkness, a pit into which he kept sinking, sinking.

CHAPTER 8

Deep in that pit of darkness presently voices were shouting; it seemed that many hands were tapping at a door. Culver wakened and thought he was in hell.

He was in a room with curving walls and a huge iron windlass in the middle, sweating with damp. He saw this through a fog and reek of tobacco smoke. He saw it through a mist, as it were, of many odors—the smell of wet rust, and sweat, and dunnage, and tar, and the sea. He knew that he was in the forecastle of a ship. The tapping was the constant pound of the waves under the prow, now one by one, now in hurried rushings.

Through this mist of smoke and stench, he saw men drunkenly swaying, shouting, singing, talking. It roared into his ears in a tumultuous babble.

" 'A hare, a parson, or a captain's wife—' " someone was singing.

Then: "Who's seen my chest? The lashings is round sennit and damn' diamond hitchin'—"

" 'Casey Jones, with a hammer in his hand—' "

"You take Star plug, it has more molasses in it—"

"Where's my chest? My God, I done them lashings over wire!"

" 'Belay that,' says the skipper, hot as hell. The square-head up and answers: 'You damn' old barnacle, belay that —sir!' The Old Man jumped right off the break of the poop and come forward with a rope's end—"

"For God's sake, where's my chest?"

Culver shook his head to clear the mist away, the fog through which the figures moved obscurely. Then he realized that his glasses were gone. They must have been smashed to flinders by the blow which had knocked him senseless.

He lifted his hand to his face. His fingertips slipped in blood. The cut ran up from between his eyes to his hair, angling to the left a little.

He took the hand down. His head began to throb with increasing pain as fuller consciousness returned to him. Then, just above him, he saw the obscure face of Joe.

"Well, you've come out of it, have you? I thought I'd cracked your skull for you. I told Burke there was no need to bash you down like that. But he's got a cockeyed idea that nobody but you could handle the damned dog. And maybe he's right. How'd you come to get so chummy with that man-eater?"

Culver thought of the senseless body in the gutter. He thought of the teeth that had closed over his arm the other night. There was no use trying to explain how he had walked the edge of a cliff of danger, so to speak, before the big fellow had accepted him as a millionaire accepts a servant. He had no words for explaining; but he said: "I must go back on shore."

"Sure, sure!" said Joe. "Sure you'll go ashore. Four or six or eight thousand miles south, you'll go ashore. Don't you worry about that, brother."

Joe disappeared, and the beating of the waves of the sea seemed to grow louder. Culver tried to think. There was no brain in his head for the effort. "Four or six or eight thousand miles south!"

But there were his books in his room. What would happen to them?

Besides, he had to see Thomas Wiley's father, the next morning, and get whatever job the charity of Sally had provided for him. He had to see her, also, and thank her again. He had not thanked her enough, the night before.

A voice roared, entering the forecastle. Mighty shoulders butted the mist aside.

"Lay all aloft and loose the sails. All hands, there! Lay aloft!" the voice was shouting.

Sails—and this was the age of steam. There could not be anything to this dream of the *Spindrift,* and the dog, and Mister, and the blow with a blackjack.

A big hand took him by the hair of the head and jerked him out of the bunk. It seemed as though the top of his head had come off, cut away by a red-hot knife.

He sat up, ready to fight. The mighty form had passed on, jerking other men out of bunks. They staggered with liquor and sleep. Some of them mumbled: "All right, bosun. Laying aloft—"

The men were crowding out from the reek of the forecastle; the bosun kicked the loiterers on their way as Culver came to his feet again. The bosun had a face like a child's, smooth and gross, the face of a fat child on top of an enormous body. "Step lively, you!" he shouted. "Lay aloft!"

"I have to go ashore—" said Culver.

He saw the blow coming, but his dim eyes could not tell how to block it. It caught him on the tip of the chin and slammed him against the wall, stunned.

"Now lay aloft, will you?" roared the bosun.

Culver staggered after the others. The foot of the bosun helped him out on deck. But there was no use trying to fight back. He kept saying that to the animal which was be-

48

ginning to rage inside him. There was no use trying to fight back through the twilight that covered his eyes. He had to be a sheep, driven by the shepherd's dog.

On deck, the sea wind cut him through his wound to the brain. Lights on either hand drifted back behind them, like glowworms in the dark hedges of an August night. That was San Francisco over there on the left. They were through the Golden Gate. The great bridge spanned the sky behind them with a single leap. The pilot-boat lay off in the near distance, and the pilot was going out to it in a small skiff. The tug which had brought the *Spindrift* out of harbor lay right ahead on the towline.

"All hands aloft!"

Culver looked up and saw against the sky the masts and the cordage like spider webs of infinite confusion. The mast heads went right up among the stars.

"Follow me, buddy," said a voice.

Culver followed, licking his lips and tasting his own blood.

He climbed the ratlines, feeling his way with hands and feet toward each separate hold, for his eyes left everything a mist. It was like a dream in which he chased a monkey through a forest in a cold, naked winter, a forest of thin shadows with branches of dimness wavering before his straining eyes.

When he reached the lubber's hole at the top of the foremast, he would have gone up through it, but the voice of his teacher called: "Don't go that way. Learn right if you're gonna learn at all. You follow Alec!"

He followed Alec, clambering out until his body hung almost horizontal above the deck, then swarming up again. Already they were a frightful distance above the deck, and the *Spindrift* was rocking in a sharp seaway.

"Now you're taking the proper sailor's road aloft," said

49

Alec. "You'll learn, but you're slow with your hands, and that's hell afloat."

"My eyes are bad," said Culver. "I've got to get ashore. I've been shanghaied. Can I get ashore?"

"Sure, somewhere in the South Seas," answered Alec. "Now look alive and be a sailor. A sailor's hands has gotta be his brains. He thinks with 'em. The sea air will fix up your eyes, all right. You watch me, and do the same things."

He followed Alec, trying to obey. But he kept saying in the emptiness of his heart: "South Seas! South Seas!"

How far that was from the study of the mysterious Etruscan past, where the voice of Etruria some day would be made to appear, perhaps, and a tongue be given to a whole dead civilization! Even the face of Mrs. Lindley began to seem friendly and full of cheer, as he remembered the life from which he had come; but chiefly there was that beautiful opportunity wasted of finding employment with the Wiley lumber company; and there were other unnamed happinesses which he felt, though he hardly could give them name and face.

He was lying across a yard that bucked and trembled like wild horses. He climbed dwindling rigging until it shook and gave unearily. He was up there in the cold, windy sky, miles above his old life, miles above the deck, so that the thought of the downward journey took the breath and the heart out of him.

There were gaskets to be loosed. Other sails were being set. The wind got into them. The lights, thinly scattered along the shore, drew off into a far immensity of radiance which with its fingertips touched the clouds. That was San Francisco. That was life. And time was sliding away beneath him like a fast-flowing river. Wasted time, weeks, perhaps months of it, stolen out of his life.

He thought of Burke, and murder came up in him.

Other blots and clots of darkness clambered in the rigging of other masts. The sails were blooming like dim flowers against the dark of the sea. Suddenly the *Spindrift* heeled over, far over, and slithered him from his foot-rope. His left hand lost its grip. He hung by the slack of a rope with his right hand only, and clawed his way back to the mast.

"I thought you were gone!" shouted Alec. "But you got a pair of hands. They may be slow, but you got a pair of hands. Once you get your feet under you, you'll make a sailor. We'll want you in the port watch. I'll tip the second mate the wink. We'll want you, brother."

The lifted voice of Burke shouted from aft: "Cast off the tug!"

Another voice in the bows roared through a megaphone: "Cast off the towline!"

The thin streak of darkness that connected the *Spindrift* with the tug, and which was the last spider thread of hope that linked Samuel Culver with the land, disappeared. Men on the forecastle began to hand in the line on the run, looping it down on the deck.

Orders shouted up to them. They went down to the deck again, Culver hurrying as he tried to keep pace with Alec. But Alec was as active in the rigging as an ape.

Now the headsails were loosed, the topgallants followed. He was hauling on ropes here, ropes there, with the elbow of Alec in his ribs from time to time to spur him on. The wind was taking them strongly. The lightship rocked away became hull down. Except for that light, the horizon was a great bowl of darkness, and through everything blew a new, thin voice of music, the wind in the rigging.

He stood idle for a moment. The sails climbed up the sky on pyramids of blue, all standing to the royals, filled with wind, and each seeming to have a separate voice, like caves of sound.

51

"Ay, look up," said Alec. "The devil himself would make a proper sailor if he would keep an eye aloft."

There was time now to stow the mooring lines; as Culver worked, the river ocean flowed beside him, and they passed out of the darkness into the dawn. He watched the sails turn lustrous apple-green like chrysoprase, then thin alabaster; but when the sea fog parted above them, letting the sun through, the sails shone like bubbles, frozen hard by the wind.

Some of the trouble went out of Culver as he watched. This was beauty such as he never had seen before; but he felt that his poets, perhaps, had seen it three thousand years before him. Perhaps the great sea song had first formed in the throat of Homer when he saw the wind lean into a sail and heard the rushing of the bow-wave.

In the excitement of the work, and the danger aloft, he had forgotten the pain of his wound; and now it seemed that the wound had forgotten him. The ache of it would have been enough to crush Culver, ashore, but at sea it was a trifling thing.

"All hands lay aft! Lay aft!"

He went with the rest, a crowd of yellow, black and white, in clothes already fingermarked with tar and grease. They had their own thoughts. Some of their glances touched the wounded forehead of Culver with casual eyes, as though it were no more than a bit of meaningless print on a page.

The crowd gathered at the after hatch of the ship. Above the break of the poop stood Burke, big, blunt-faced, red of neck. A litle round man with a jolly face walked up and down the deck behind him, the only person who moved on the ship as Burke stood there, surveying the crowd.

"There goes Jimmy Green," said Alec, whispering at Culver's shoulder. "Damn him and double damn the rotten swine! Now hark at the Old Man. That's what Burke is, aboard this ship, now that Valdez has gone out of it."

Culver put the name of Valdez away in his memory for future reference. Burke spoke. His voice was deep, but somehow there was a high whine in it, like a bull terrier working at a grip.

"I'm gonna say something to the whole of you," he called out. "It's something important. A lot of you are new, and it won't mean much to you, part of what I say. But the old crew will understand. The rest of you, lay it down, frame it, timber it, and calk it tight, because it's the idea that we're sailing by.

"I'm talking about a fellow named Walter Toth. Some of the old crew ought to remember him. They remember the day when we picked him out of the water up at Juneau, a couple of years back. They remember that he was hell-bent on getting to the South Seas to pick up a whole backload of pearls. They remember that they got half drunk and staked him with cash, to make the try, and he was going to give us our split. Well, I won't tell you the whole story. The rest of the boys will tell you that. All I say to the new part of the crew is that you get double pay if the job comes off. And to the old crew, I say that we split up our part of the swag even all around, unless you want to vote extra shares for your officers. Walter Toth is out there dying; and some of us think we know where he lies. We're going out there to hunt for him. It's no easy job. It's hard, because everybody that's up against Chinee Valdez is up against something hard."

He paused. Like a sound of the wind, low and complaining, a groan came out of many throats. It came from Alec along with the rest. That name of Valdez took on a new meaning, for Culver.

CHAPTER 9

Someone else appeared on the poop—a girl with golden-brown skin, her black hair done in a knot at the back of her neck. She wore a dress of faded blue stripes with a red cord knotted around her waist. The wind leaned against her, and she did not have on many clothes. But she stood with her fists on her hips and her legs spread to the pitching of the deck and her head raised to look at the sails. It was plain that she did not care what eyes looked at her. She was free as a boy; she had a boy's pride about her.

Burke passed into another theme. He said: "Chinee Valdez is on the sea now, or he'll soon be, and we're going to try to be on his heels. And if we ever cross his wake, we've got his dog to follow 'im! I've seen to that!"

A quick, deep murmur came from Alec and others. They were pleased by this news. And Culver, at last, had the name of the dog's master: Chinee Valdez, former skipper of the *Spindrift*. As though to give point to the new skipper's talk, the dog they called Napico came out on the poop to the very break of it, and stood looking straight ahead along their course, with the wind pulling his thick tail to one side and ruffling his deep hair. When he looked down, he favored the crew in the waist with a silent grimace of hatred that showed his fangs.

Against this background Burke was saying: "But we've got to cut corners and we've got to save time. The *Spindrift* is an old one. She leaks. She groans and she whispers, but she's a lady. No faster set of lines were ever drawn to carry sails. Sails ain't steam, but we're going to make them come damn' close. I'm going to sail her. I'm going to crack on if I have to blow the damned tophamper out of her rotten keelson: I'm telling you, the men that help get double pay; but if you soldier, by God, I'll eat your hearts. . . . Lay forward, men!"

The wind held for them as they went south. It held day after day. Culver grew a set of blisters, broke them, hardened his hands anew. Twice he nearly fell to his death from aloft when his dim eyes made him miss a grip; but he was beginning now to get the feel of things aloft.

He had expected, after the new skipper's talk, that he would hear a great buzz of conversation, but Burke worked them so hard, constantly trimming sail, constantly adding and shortening it as the wind permitted, that the men were too tired for talk until the last whisky dregs had worked out of their bodies. He himself, in spite of his good trim, had every labor doubled by the dimness of his eyes, so that as a rule he had to fumble twice before he was sure of any handhold. But he was almost glad of the fatigue, because it gave him no opportunity to think about the books which he had left to the tender mercies of Mrs. Lindley. Perhaps— and the thought froze his brain—perhaps she would sell them at once, and they would be scattered over the whole wide face of the world!

That was why he dared not think back, but tried to house himself closely in every moment of his work.

He talked very little to anyone; for the rest of the crew, except Alec, despised him. It was because he had accepted the blow and the kick of the bosun, Jemmison, without an effort to fight back, that they looked down upon him. They sent him to run errands; they ordered him to bring the bucket of tea from the galley. And after that, they turned their backs upon him.

Respect from such a collection of gutter rats was hardly to be desired, perhaps; yet this constant contempt bit into the very marrow of his bones. Even Alec, who looked upon him with a sort of fondness as an adopted pupil, observed once just within earshot of Culver: "A guy that has bad eyes, it takes the guts out of him!"

"It seems a hard ship," Culver said to Alec. "The crew is hard, and the officers are hard on them."

"I'll tell you something, and you button your lip down close on top of it," said Alec: "This ain't America; this ain't England; this ain't Finland, or Greenland, or Iceland, either. This is Valdez-land. This here is his house—and there's his pasture lands, kind of bluer than grass, and there's white sheep winkin' in and out."

He indicated the wide ocean, and the frothing crests of the waves.

"This is Valdez-land," he repeated. "And don't you forget it. Some of these dummies think that Burke is only a shadow of the Old Man, but they'll find out different. Burke has swiped the Valdez ship. To follow Valdez, he swipes Valdez' ship, and that's piracy or something. Burke knows it. The rest of us are in the soup with Burke; some of us old hands are, anyway; but Burke would have to take the main rap. And he knows that. One of these mugs is goin' to speak out of turn, one day, and Burke'll turn him inside out by way of an object lesson."

"Who is the girl?" asked Culver.

"Koba? She's none of my damned business," answered Alec; "nor yours, neither. She's something that Valdez picked up down south of nowhere, and thought she'd make cabin furniture. But she fooled him. And if she fooled Valdez, I guess she could fool anybody else. You keep your eyes off of her. She's poison."

"Have you sailed much with Valdez, Alec?" asked Culver.

56

"Yeah. I put in some time with him."

"Where did you sail?"

"Aw, in the China Seas, and south of that, and south of that, and south to sugar palms and hell, if you want to know. Chinee Valdez is his parlor name. Old South is what we call him, me and Sibu and all the rest that stick with him: Elia, and all the old hands."

"What's the story about Walter Toth and the pearls?" asked Culver.

"Toth? Pearls?" answered Alec. "I wouldn't know anything about that!" And he broke off the talk.

By this time they had the ship in good trim. All on deck was shipshape; all aloft was in good order. On a fair wind they blew southward and westward. Culver lay in his bunk one afternoon when his watch was below and listened to the slop of water at the bows and felt her lift and fly. When he thought of the *Spindrift* by herself, it seemed as though she could overtake any other man-made invention, but then he had to remember that she was living now in a different age, for which she was not meant. But he had an odd feeling that she was carrying him to his destiny. Napico, the dog, had led him to her, and now she was taking him south toward Valdez. In his soul, Culver had not the slightest doubt that eventually he would see the dog's master face to face. And then something would happen. Something strange—though he could not put tongue nor mind to it. . . .

He saw the dog only now and again on the quarter-deck, where he roamed, and paid no heed to the crew. People who walked the quarter-deck were safe from his teeth, the sailors said, so long as they did not blunder into him. *Napico,* meant, they said, "Does not bite. ("Not much he don't bite!" said Alec.)

The seasick days were gone behind Culver, now. His belly was as gaunt and hard as iron. The blisters on his hands had changed to calluses, and there was another change which he hardly dared admit to himself. Either he had become so familiar with the rigging that he knew his way about, or else his eyes actually were better, so much better that sometimes a queer hope rose up in him that they might return entirely to normal. That, after all, was what the oculist had promised him, if ever he gave them a complete rest.

He was in his bunk now, because the other men did not like to have him with them. They sprawled in various attitudes; Alec, squat as an ape, with red freckles showing through the brown of his face, said: "Give us a song, Constantine, you little damn' Caruso—give us a song, will you?"

Then Constantine the Greek sat up and looked around him with glimmering eyes. He was American by force of trade, having grown from a bootblack to a thief, and from a thief to a sailor.

"Give me a tune," he said. "Elia—hey, Francolini! Give me a tune, and I'll put words to it."

Francolini was an Italian with a face as sour as sour wine. He was of the "old crew," who had something more than wages to hope for out of this cruise. He drew a harmonica from his pocket, and without a word, as though he preferred giving in, to arguing with a detested Greek, he blew a few notes to find himself, and then struck up an old air.

Constantine, the beautiful young Greek, sang in a husky tenor:

Come all you young sailormen, listen to me;
I'll sing you a song of the fish in the sea.
Then blow the winds westerly, westerly blow;
We're bound to the southward, so steady she goes.

Oh, first come the whale, the biggest of all.
He climbed up aloft and let every sail fall.
And next come the mackerel with his striped back.
He hauled aft the sheets and boarded each tack.

And next come a Dyak from Borneo
By name of Sibu, and he said: "Let her go!"

There was a chuckle among the men at this mention of one of the watch. Sibu was one of Valdez' old crew. He looked up and favored them all with a grin. But the grin had no meaning, and while his lips were twitched back, his eyes ran like cats from face to face to study the expressions. They were careful how they looked, when Sibu was watching them like that.

Constantine, having started the theme, went on with swift improvisation to develop it, striking in at will into the sing-song music of Francolini.

There was gold in his teeth and gold in his grin;
The smile that was in him, he couldn't keep in.
He wore a bandana instead of a hat
And he liked to go bare. What's the matter with that?

He wore a brass ring; he talked Yankee slang;
He swore like a Christian; he prayed to Sang Sang.
He prayed to Sang Sang but he worshiped a skull,
And he kept his knife sharp and he kept his eyes dull.
He liked his meat high and he liked his winds low,
But a thirst in his throat made him yell:
        "Let her go!"

The watch laughed a little at the description, and Sibu laughed with them, but his eyes were always veiled, and waiting to find trouble and ready for it. Culver realized with a slight shudder that he had just heard the description of a head-hunting native. Perhaps Sibu had eaten some strange kinds of meat, in his time, thought Culver.

Constantine was now in the full flair of improvisation, and he continued with his singing: Alec, the Frenchman Latour, the Italian Francolini, the Southerner George Green, the smugly smiling Englishman Will Carman—one by one the improviser impaled them, lampooned them with a crude and bitter humor.

The savage Irishman, O'Doul, was the next victim. The sound of his name roused him the way a whip stroke might rouse an Irish horse. He was swearing slowly through scarcely moving lips as he listened.

> Then come the O'Doul with his Irish lies,
> A terrier's jaws and a terrier's eyes.
> He had hunted the lowland and hunted the hill;
> He had ridden the silk and looked at the kill.
> He talked of the green but he thought of the red,
> And he took to ships to keep from his dead.

Here Constantine, out of breath or out of ideas, made a longer pause than before, and Culver felt the rising anger at work in his victims. He expected at any moment to hear a voice raised, cursing.

It was perfectly plain that Constantine understood the danger, and yet he seemed to enjoy the taste of fear that it put in his threat. He had grown a little pale, but his eyes burned with a savage delight as he scanned his victims.

Then the danger came to a sudden head in the slow, steady rising of Latour, the Frenchman; and Sibu was stealing up to his knees also, his smile never stopping.

Constantine suddenly struck into a verse that brought his chant to an end. As he began, Latour and Sibu slipped back into position, their eyes still hungrily fixed upon the singer. Gradually their expressions changed as they listened. For the singer had lifted his voice to a louder tone as he began:

Then Constantine came, and he sung a gay note
With the tar on his hands and the fog in his throat.
He waited for others, before he talked;
He went behind, when the lions walked.
His ways they were gentle; his manner was meek;
And he kissed the fist like a God-damned Greek!

Constantine, as he reached the definite ending of the song and himself, lay back on his elbows and breathed deeply, his lips sneering, and his eyes on the alert; but his last lines had pleased his audience so entirely that they guffawed happily and loudly. Only Alec, the best-natured of them all, said when he had finished laughing: "But some day I'm gonna poke you on your dago chin, you Constantine!"

Rogers, the cabin steward, came down into the forecastle just then. He was a long and lean pink-jowled Englishman who walked around with his eyes closed and a partial smile on his lips as though he were meditating a secret with a jest in it.

He said: "I been hearing something. I been hearing plenty!"

They forgot Constantine and stared at Rogers. He liked to come down among the men, and they liked to have him, because he brought them news of what was happening among the afterguard.

"What do you think of the mate?" said Rogers. "What d'you think?"

He could not continue his story. He had to taste his own news again and swallow on it, smiling again in inward enjoyment.

"How the hell should we know what to think? What's up now?" asked Alec.

"He wants Koba!" said Rogers. "He's after Koba!"

Nobody spoke, but several of the old crew grinned. They

liked this tidbit.

"Valdez couldn't get that she-devil, but Burke is trying his hand. I heard him."

"What did he say?" someone asked. "How the hell did he go about it?"

"What he said don't matter much. It's what she said that counts," answered Rogers. "She said: 'Go and grow—grow as big as Jemmison! He's the most man on this ship. I wouldn't have anybody but the most man!' "

"Jemmison—the bosun! She wants Jemmison!" shouted Latour, the Frenchman. "She wants Jemmison. The good God! That's why she wouldn't have Valdez himself. She ain't got brain enough. She thinks Jemmison is the most man because there's more of him. Because he has the strongest back!"

Then Alec said: "Jemmison—that hog-face! He could have her."

He said it softly and sadly, with something of a childish wonder in his voice.

"Jemmison!" repeated two or three of the others, looking at each other with blankly speculative eyes.

CHAPTER 10

They logged on south and south. One evening Culver was summoned aft to Burke, walking the poop. They had electric lights in the cabin, served by a small dynamo. The steady radiance in the companionway was pleasant. It was the first time Culver had been aft, for Burke would not have a green hand at the wheel while the wind served and the

62

Spindrift was logging like a lady.

Burke said: "You got it rather rough, Culver. It was a kind of a dirty trick I played on you in Frisco."

Culver listened in a faint surprise. It was apparent that the captain wished to be conciliatory. Far more important to Culver was the fact that even through the dimness of the twilight he could read the features of the skipper and see his half-sneering, half-amiable smile. He had not dreamed that his eyes had improved as much as this!

When he made no remark except, "Yes, sir," Burke went on: "You got a kind of a brain in your head."

"I hope so, sir," said Culver, mildly.

"You got a brain you could think something through with," said the complimentary skipper. "Now I wanta know, did you ever know anything about wireless?"

Culver remembered that he had seen the layout of Tommy Wiley. It would be incorrect to say that he was absolutely ignorant.

"I can't say that I know nothing at all," he answered.

"Good!" exclaimed Burke heartily. "That's talking up like a man. Damned good! I'll tell you what: I'm going to give you a chance at an easy job. The only hand on board that ever knew anything about the radio was Valdez. Damn him, he was too smart to have any other operator. He didn't want any pair of ears on the ship listening in on him when he talked over the air. He wanted the key all to himself. Now, I want you to go down there and take a look at that radio and see can you do something with it. This way, Culver."

The radio room was no larger than a good-sized closet. It had been sealed up all through the voyage, and the air was dead in it, and full of the sweat of iron, and the odor of decaying grease. The radio itself presented a confused tangle to Culver.

He said: "I don't know enough to—"

"Sure you don't know enough to sit right down to it," said Burke. "But you get it all together and figure it out. . . . Look out! There comes Napico."

The big dog was slinking toward Culver through the dusk.

"Jump for the break of the poop!" shouted Burke. "Jump, or he'll tear your throat out. It's better to break a leg than have your throat cut open!"

Culver stood still.

"Jump, you damn' fool!" roared Burke. "He won't stand a sailor aft, except at the wheel or on the way to it! Jump!"

Culver stood still. The dog came up and sniffed at the trouser pocket in which the ebony cross was carried. Culver laid a hand on his head and felt the huge body grow stiff with resentment; he felt the tremor rather than heard the sound of the snarl that bubbled in that throat. Then the snarling died out; he stroked the head of Napico, and the dog continued to sniff at the pocket.

"That's funny!" said Burke. "Bar Valdez, I never seen him go that far with anybody. What did you ever do to that crazy hellion, anyway? What did you feed him?"

Culver was silent, petting the dog. He felt that he should explain that in the cross he carried a charm which the big brute hardly could withstand, and yet he felt the explanation would be too long.

"All right. Go forward," said Burke. "But when tomorrow gets the sun up, you come back here and start rigging up that radio, will you? And cheer up, Culver."

Culver went forward.

"What kind of hell did the old man give you?" asked Alec. "I never heard him talk so soft to anybody. What kind of hell did he give you?"

"Not very much," answered Culver. For again it would

have been too hard to explain.

And afterward he heard Francolini saying to George Green in a hush between gusts of wind: "I was up in the foreshrouds, and I seen it. The dog come snooping. 'Jump!' says Mister. He just stood; he didn't jump. And Pico come up and stood like a lamb and gave his head to Culver's hand. Gave his head to that yellow-bellied rat!"

George Green said: "Nobody can understand dogs. Nobody can understand women. So why try?"

"But it took guts, just to stand there, didn't it?" asked Francolini.

Then the wind came, rubbing the rest of that talk out of Culver's ears. . . .

Every day he worked on the radio now, except when all hands were called in a squall, now and then. There was a chart and a code book. Since nobody else on board had the slightest idea of what electricity meant, it was as well to apply his mind to the subject as to confess his real ignorance. By degrees he built up his understanding, photographing the details, recombining them in his brain, until the subject began to take clear form. But it was slow work, and he was in a fog all the time, a fog that gradually thinned. Burke let him alone, content to see him bending over the instrument for hours each day; and every day his eyes were clearer; every day he fumbled less among the wires and the small instruments. In off moments he practiced with the buzzer, sending to nothingness.

They were far out now. The *Spindrift* was not a summer hotel, and the food was bad. The salt beef was hard; the lumps of pork turned green in the steep-tank water; the weevils already had honeycombed the ancient biscuit; it was necessary to give the hardtack a few taps to clear each piece before it was put into the mouth.

They had to man the pumps in every watch, working the

bilges dry through a long, long damnation of labor. Some of the crew said that she had sprung a leak and that the first storm would send her down. The winds were very light now. They were rigging studdingsails constantly, or taking them in when the gusts blew. Reefing and bracing, setting and striking canvas, they nursed her tenderly along every wind, with Burke growing thin on the poop, and cursing every move that was made, no matter how expertly the crew responded to orders.

But they forgave him for his brutal treatment, because they knew that he was matching the days of the *Spindrift* against the days of some unseen steamer, hull-down on the horizon, that carried Valdez toward the undoing of their hopes.

Exactly what it was that Valdez had in hand, Culver could not gather, except from the first speech that Burke had made to his crew. But there were pearls—pearls that a Walter Toth had found; and Toth was the wandering relative of Sally Franklin; and the crew had a certain right to them; and Valdez was bent on taking them all for himself; and the *Spindrift* was to fumble among the South Sea Islands in order to cross the trail of Valdez, which might lead them to their goal; and the dog Napico might help them if ever they found the fresh trail of the dog's master.

This story, after all, was reasonably clear. Only the details were lacking from it. It carried an immense irony, in that Valdez' own ship was being used to run him down, and the dog of Valdez was their ace in the hole. And sometimes it seemed to Culver that there was something fated and pre-destined for him in this whole structure of events, with his discharge at the express office as the opening moment, and the dog as the leading dramatic impulse which wove to-gether the girl, the wireless, the ebony cross, the *Spindrift*, and worked him into the pattern of a strange new existence.

66

He had time to ponder these things as he worked in the radio room. The rest of the crew, during the doldrums which came, were kept at work aloft, tarring down the rigging spun yarn, serving, parceling, reeving off new gear.

Culver learned much about everyone, as time went on. For his memory, like the shutter of a fast camera, clicked on every word, every expression, filing the crowds of images away in his mind; and on that material his brain could not help working, like the scholarly instrument that it was, filling in gaps, deducing, constructing, fitting the whole characters together out of small parts, in large acts of synthesis. He was without his books, but he remained a student, with men instead of pages to pore over when he was away from the radio room. Then one day he hooked up the instrument in his mind, not in fact, and knew that he had it right. The next morning he switched on the current, and the receiver began to jerk out messages. It was a moment of strange importance. The world which had been taken from him was now restored, dimly and far away, like something seen through a telescope of high power. The face of things was gone, but a strange voice could reach him.

Then they struck a calm. They drifted. And as they hung there with the sails slatting against the masts, something— a ghost, a whisper—seemed to be overtaking them; something was moving toward them over the curving cheek of the ocean.

It was fiercely hot; sun poured on the ship, flaking the paint away as though with a blowpipe. The tar boiled in the seams. Within the tanks the water slowly reddened; blood seemed to be dripping into it day by day. And the masts were nailed solidly against the sky. The sails no longer stirred. They hung down with ever-deepening lines, like human faces growing old. The helmsman leaned on the useless wheel.

Culver endured it very well. Thin fare for many years made it easy for him to accept the positively bad fare of the *Spindrift*; and in the doldrums he was allowed for the first time to take the wheel and con the ship through the rising and dying winds, always studying the tremor in the leeches as he held her close up to each breath.

It was the most exciting physical event of his life. Before that, he simply was on the ship. But at the wheel, he held her in his hand. She belonged to him. For him she luffed her head around. For him the very wind sang in the cordage. She was his. He could not help an amazing sense of gratitude to the *Spindrift* because she obeyed him so implicitly. And then, as he stood there, he had a pleasant sense that many eyes were watching. They were not on him, though the second mate had told him, with a few blunt oaths, that he had a knack for steering, but they were observing because when he went aft, the big dog came out and sat down beside him, turning his head with apparent companionable friendliness to him again and again. But Culver knew it was because of the scent of the ebony cross which was always in his pocket. Sometimes, toward the end of his trick at the wheel, Napico would lie down at his feet and remain there, motionless but apparently happy.

And now, when he went forward, the dog formed the habit of following him all the way to the break of the poop and staring after him until he had disappeared from the deck.

"He's got something on the dog," said Francolini. "He knows something about Napico, and the dog hopes that he won't tell the rest of us!"

Then came utter calm, the windless hours, the windless days, the windless nights, and a tension began to build up in the whole crew, and in the whole ship, so it seemed to Culver, as though the *Spindrift* lived with a set of nerves which could feel human suspense, and the need to get places on time.

Sometimes Koba came out and looked at him for a brief moment, and then forgot his presence. She would look at him from head to foot, and then at the dog, and then turn away. It was plain to Culver that she wanted to understand what it was in him that attracted the great dog; and not understanding, she returned again and again to the problem.

He enjoyed having her on the deck because she was like a pretty picture. The golden brown of her skin made the sea bluer and the canvas whiter. When she moved, she made motion beautiful and effortless, and there was a sort of rhythm about everything she did, as though she were doing it to music. She was very young. In time maternity and too-early maturity would sweep over her in a tide of flesh. He had seen pictures of South Sea Island girls and matrons many a time, and he knew what the future held for her. But at the moment she was as trim as a yearling filly, which is one of the most beautiful works of God. Her face lacked that finish and delicate modeling which only comes to an intellectual race, as though the mind worked to refine the features, but she had the loveliness of a beautiful animal.

It was not Koba that he paid most attention to, however, when he stood at the wheel. The handling of the ship gave him quite another companion, and that sense of spiritual possession which he felt when the *Spindrift* changed her course, obedient to the spokes he turned on the wheel, led him somehow to another visualization: He kept seeing Sally Franklin just beyond the corner of his eye. Sometimes he asked himself if this were the beginning of an absurd infatu-ation—a man of thirty-five losing his head about a young girl; but as a matter of fact, it was rather, he thought, an association of ideas. Sally Franklin was almost never in his mind except when he stood at the helm of the *Spindrift,* and then something about the thoroughbred, slender grace of the ship reminded him of the girl. At any rate, those hours at the helm were by far his happiest hours on the ship, and he left the wheel unhappily when he returned to the radio room.

He heard a strange tale one evening during the calms. He was through his watch in the radio room. The sun lay on his belly in the west, puffing his cheeks and blowing flames and purple smoke across the sea. The crew gathered on the forecastle head for a yarn.

A school of flying fish on twittering wings flew past the sun in streaks of rose and amber, and after them the dolphins came leaping, as azure as the sea, but dripping with crimson and gold and green. Their beauty like a wind freshened the eyes of Culver.

"She's got her chin in the mud," said Dutchy, who was the ship's Sails.

"She's old!" answered George Green.

"Her heart is young enough," said Rory O'Doul, "but too much asking has tired her."

The sailors nodded, listening to the rasping parrals, the clanking of the pump and the gush of water as the other watch labored.

"But whether she runs or rests, she's always drinking," said Constantine.

"Oh, God, blast her bloody heart, how she will sop it up if a storm hits her!" commented the Englishman.

"It's lying still and looking at the sun that makes her thirsty," said Latour.

"Shut up," said Alec. "Stop the grouching. Where's a story? Elia, give us a yarn from Dago-land."

"When I was whaling, boys—," said a deep, powerful voice."

That was the cook; he was a big Negro. Some people said

70

that he was almost stronger than Jemmison, the bosun.

"When I was whaling—," he began.

"Oh, God," said George Green, "he's gonna tell his tale again—how he met Chinee Valdez. He's like a fly stuck in one drop of glue on one spider thread, that'll buzz and buzz the same damn' story till the spider eats him. That's what I'll do, some hungry day. Doctor, go on. But if you change one word of the yarn, if you start anything new in it and wake me up, I'll throw you overboard."

He stretched himself out on a coil of rope, a coil of big line that cradled him from neck to knees.

"Go on with the yarn," he said. "Start with the *Murmurer*."

CHAPTER 11

What Culver heard was fact and legend and emotion so oddly blended that it was difficult to tell where one began and another took on.

"The *Murmurer!*" said Peterson. "There was a ship! A clipper is a lady, but a whaler is a man with double timbers that never hog or sag. Ice couldn't bust the *Murmurer*. It never whimpered because of the sea or him that drove the ship. That was Parrish, boys. Red Parrish was getting old. Mostly his hair was gone, except a fringe. But all of him was red and yellow-freckled, blistered and peeling. Parrish—he was a cat, and the fat mice he hunted around the world was sperm whales. He ran them in the attic to Baffin Bay. He ran them in the basement to South Shetlands and the Weddell Sea. He could have found them in the dark, smelling them out. His eyes were always bloodshot, and he sniffed like he was smelling blood always, too. Though the hold was full, Parrish was never full. He damned and slammed us. Half of every crew signed for the hope of seeing Parrish die. The carpenter, he waited out seven cruises. This was an easy passage, the one I'm talking about: the Bermudas, the two Thirty-sixes. Then we swung around the world from Madagascar east to Fiji and the Friendly Isles. We looked in sunshine at the Horn. The dirty devil showed us his bald head and the teeth he eats with. There was a cold wind out of the south, darkening and wrinkling the sea, and putting beards on the big rollers, and we climbed up the hills and slid down the valleys; and a lookout yells out of the fore rigging—"

"Damn you, Doctor," said George Green, "you know you left out something back there—about the waves you were climbing."

"So I did," said Peterson. "I guess I sure did leave something out. I should have said those hills and valleys in the sea were as sleek as gray iron. Then a lookout yells out of the fore rigging: 'A sail! A small boat on the weather bow! Ahoy the deck! A small sail on the weather bow!'

"We thought he'd mistook the white chin whiskers of an old roller for the shine of canvas. Those waves were heavier than melted iron. They kept four hundred tons of us a-bobbing, so what could small boats do, how could they live in such a seaway? But then we saw, out of the southward, like something that had crept up from the Pole, something that was running like a deer across the hills and valleys of the water. It was a dory. Just a dory, mind you! A damned little bob-nosed dory, and a snatch of sail with only one man showing in the stern sheets. We all stood by to shorten sail. Says Chips: 'It's Davy Jones, coming to get his pay from Parrish; and that cash is a long time overdue.' And by God, that devil Parrish, instead of bringing the ship to, he hollers to lay her off a point or two; and then he sings out to get the topgallants on her."

"Was he scared, Doctor?" asked Alec.

"Well," said the cook, "I'll admit that it had a lonely look, that one man and the dory jumping in the wind. We got the lashings off the main topgallant, but as the ship started running, the little dory ran up the weather side of the wave we were riding and threw its man aboard. Then it fell flat and went drifting away on its side, as though it was tired of living, and ready to go back home after doing this job for Davy Jones. Right there among us stands the castaway.

"Parrish, like the old devil that he was, shows his teeth as he looks on. But this castaway, this young devil—because that's what he looked like with his big beak of a nose and his chin sticking out, and his eyes and his hair as black as the pit of the night—he stood there and only laughed. All we got out of him was that his name was Valdez."

Peterson made a pause, when he reached this point in his story. As though he knew that he had touched on a charm which would hold his audience as long as he chose, he deliberately prolonged the silence while he filled a pipe and lighted it. He smacked his lips, getting up a head of fire in the bowl of the pipe. When he had it drawing well, he said: "He bunked with us forward and turned to in the starboard watch like any common sailor. He never talked. What ship that dory was from, he never would say. All we got out of him was his name. He was three men on a rope; and he was as good as four standing on a bucking footrope and furling frozen canvas. No, he never told us how he came adrift, but he talked now and then of China and the South Seas; and he called himself Valdez. And his hair was black and his eyes were as black as his hair."

"What did you think of him?" ventured Culver.

"We knew that we'd picked some trouble off the sea,"

said the cook. "But we were happy, rounding on the Falklands, because we were full, and thought we'd done with gurry, and all that. Our harness was put away and we were fixed to settle. We'd started tons and tons of water over the side and filled with oil, and nothing remained where we could stow oil except a little corner that would fill out of the melons of a pod of blackfish. We'd finished singing: 'Five and forty more!' W'd found our luck and boiled it. Five had laid beside us in a single cut. We'd trailed the stink of burning scrap around the world since we first got off soundings. Now it was a frolic on a tow-line to Callao Grounds without a lookout.

"But one day it was me that seen right from the deck, and I sung out by habit: 'Blows! There she white-waters! Gai!' And the rest of the crew mumbled, because they didn't have any more belly for fishing: 'Ay, blows!' They mumbled it, and they watched the spouting, fifteen to the minute. You know you tell the length of a whale by the number of times that he spouts. About fifteen to a minute is the way they breathe. And the length is one foot to each breath. We were counting the spouts to ourselves until they got up to seventy. What was a big whale to us? It would have been a waste. We only had a spare corner that needed filling; we were full enough already. We should have left something for Davy Jones, they say. Anyway, when the count got up to seventy, everybody started shouting out: 'And one, and two, and three and four, and five makes seventy-five!' "

"That's a hell of a big whale, ain't it?" someone asked.

"What you think we were using our mouths for bellowing out the count, if it wasn't a big whale?" demanded the cook.

Sure it was a big whale. I've heard talk about hundred-footers, but I guess they never came that big in sperm. Not

74

in cachalots. Anyway, we had to keep right on singing out the count, because the spouting didn't stop. And pretty soon we were yelling at the top of our lungs: 'Eighty-five and eighty-six, eighty-seven, eighty-eight—make it ninety, brother!—eighty-nine, and ninety! Ninety! It was a ninety-footer. Just even. He stopped spouting, that old bull, right at ninety, even. God, a ninety-footer! I remember looking around, and the crew was all gaping and grinning with their scurvy-yellow teeth.

"Parrish, he looked to windward—to leeward was the whale—pondering on his short lay, smelling the cocks, I guess, like a horse turning homeward that has the sweet and the comfort of the manger in his nostrils. But out there the whale, like he was playing with us and waving good-by—like he knew that we were a full ship and that he was safe from us, he started lobtailing now. With a thirty-foot tail he started the thunder cracking, slamming the sea right and left. Parrish couldn't stand it. 'Clear away!' he yells.

"We rubbed our chins and stared, I'll tell you. What'd he mean, we wondered—for we was full; the boiling of his tail would of overflowed us. But it wasn't oil Parrish wanted; it was a fight to warm his hands and his damned heart inside him, if he had a heart. We all were groaning, but that other devil, that black young one, Valdez, he started laughing. He was still laughing while he helped us clear the laundry from the davits and tapped home the boat-plugs, and cast off the gripes, and loaded the line-tubs in, and cleared the falls. Three boats of us hit the water. Valdez pulled an oar in mine; and in the bows of that same boat was Parrish standing. So I had the two of them right under my eyes, and that's why I know what I'm talking about when I tell you this yarn.

"I remember that Parrish was standing in an undershirt of blue, and the blue was washed out of it in streaks because he wouldn't buy a thing for himself except old clothes, the mean old devil! And his bald head shone, and the last of his red hair, it was blowing out like a ship's flag. Then he turned around and seen Valdez, and he yelled out: 'Who in hell let that black devil into my boat!'

"He said just that, and no more. But when one devil calls another by name, you sort of know that there is a hell, and fire in it too. The look of Parrish, too, was like he had seen a devil. But now we were getting close up, and all at once Parrish gives the word. We sprang on the oars, and pretty soon we were in the slick of the oily, quiet water near the whale. He wasn't like a beast with life in it. He was like a big ship turned keel up. Then he sounded, and threw his tail half a block in the sky, and was gone.

"Parrish held us on our oars with the way on the boat stopped.

" 'Sub silentio!' Parrish says. It shows how good I remember, that I remember those words. Somebody tells me that they're Latin and mean keep your goddam mouth shut. Latin! That Parrish—that pig had Latin in his belly! It shows he'd gone away back in his mind. Back to his school days, eh? The biggest whale he'd ever seen in a life of whaling. And he was there to gaff the life out of it! And everything stopped for him; and the Latin, it comes dripping out of his mouth without knowing why.

" 'Sub silentio!' Parrish says. Then I seen a shadow rise. A mountain, not a fish. He broached so close to us that I seen the crust of barnacles along his jaw. He went on up like an elevator was hoisting him. He come down crash. The splash of him went up so high I seen the sun through it, and the sun looked silver, like a moon; and then we started on into the leaping of the white water, and finished off nose to blackskin while the first spout was snoring up. Old Parrish hitched his body back, and he bent over double, and he

76

fleshed his iron up to the hitches. And he grabbed the second iron on the short warp and sank that one too, before he gave us the sign and we backed; we'd held on so long near that mass of black that when the signal came, we leaped the boat astern. And he cut fluke. The misery was so deep in him, it pinched him so, that he skipped our bows with half a ton of tail; and then he sounded fast. The rope flew out of the Flemish coils; and every coil jumped up by itself and sang with its own voice. We had that rope good and free, but the bows of the boat sank to the water's edge with the friction. The chocks were groaning and smoking.

" 'Is he lead?' said Parrish. 'Is he never going to stop sounding?'

"Well, there was hardly twenty fathoms in the last tub when he stopped sounding and the bows staggered up. We were gathering in armfuls of the line when that old bull came butting up into the air once more. He was vomiting out tentacles of squid, a boatload to a bite. Then he ran. He done twenty knots if I ever watched a wake. That was a real Nantucket sleigh ride, boys. Like tipping over the rim and sliding down the shoulders of the sea, until we were hollow inside from the speed of it, d'you see? We were flying in a fog. The water from the piggins drove to rain. And then we stopped to a wallow.

"All the while I'd been feeling that the danger was not so much from the whale as it was from Parrish in front of me, and Valdez behind. I didn't know what that danger would be, but I damned well wished that I was back on the *Murmurer*."

It came to Culver that the cook was old. He had seemed, until this moment, not more than fifty. But now even in the dim streaking of the lantern light he looked gray on the cheeks as well as gray on the head; time had tarnished more than the mere surface of him. Perhaps he was seventy. And to get back to such whale fishing as this, Valdez must be well on in years. Could such things have been very much nearer than thirty years away?

The cook went on: "The bull, off there, was pitch-poling in the water with smoke around his head like a volcano just rising. Parrish turns around and points a finger over my head at Valdez.

" 'You—you blackhead—you, Valdez,' says Parrish. 'It's you he's smelling.'

" 'Not me,' says Valdez. 'You're hung a little higher than I am. You're riper meat.'

"I could of laughed at that, but Parrish was mad. 'I'll thrice you up, for that,' he says. 'I'll give you sixty lashes!'

"And then Valdez rose and pointed. 'There he comes. He heard you talk, and he's coming for you. He's the grandfather of all the little whales you've ever killed, Captain, and he's going to take it out of your hide!' says Valdez.

"Well, it looked that way, to see the whale come smashing along, and the big bow wave that was throwing up in front of him. Like he was lifting his head as he ran, and making sure where he was going.

"Parrish, he got into a regular crazy fit. He started to shake his fist at the whale. 'Come on, baby,' he sings out. 'I'll have another dance with you, and then I'll take you home with me and put you to bed. I'll put you to bed, and I'll put you to sleep!'

"That whale, he had his head right up, and he came humping along the water, let me tell you, boys! And the pair of waves was galloping at his bows. I've been in Cadiz and seen the bullfighter waiting for the bull with a sword. That's how we waited, and Parrish up there in the bows with a lance in his hand. Like the matador, was the way we side-stepped, too. The steering oar squealed on the steering brace, and that long wall of black went by us like the side of a train, a regular express. Parrish boned that lance and sank another. 'The flag!' said Parrish, screeching it. 'I've put a waif on him!' The bull was on his side, like a ship heeling. He was in his flurry. That last lance had touched the inside of him right in the center of where he lived. He circled as he flurried, with his mouth open. You think about twenty foot of jaw, and you can think what his mouth was like when it was open. A 'couple of barn doors. And his lower jaw was set with teeth like the spikes they used to hold down iron rails.

"He was blind and crazy. And yet he seemed to be seeing us out of his little eyes. He leaped his tail out of the water away off there. He swung it. The flukes came shining and big as the side of a house. He was taking a fair crack at us, but he was too anxious to smack us flat, and he missed. Those flukes went by in a blur of speed and a roar like a train passing. The wind of them pretty near knocked me down. But we weren't touched. The flukes went by, and we were all sitting there safe, and nobody touched at all. And then I saw that the bows of the boat were empty. Parrish was gone. That whale had come for him, like Valdez said, and the whale had took him, too. Pinched him out of the boat with thumb and forefinger, like you might say. And somehow it seemed like it was the doing of that black devil Valdez, who'd picked out the old red devil Parrish, and chucked him away to hell and gone.

"We never saw Parrish no more. The fish never saw him no more, either, except maybe them that crawl on the bottom of the sea."

Peterson stopped. The engine of his brain was laboring up a grade of thought that was difficult for him.

"Blood is one color, fish or man," said Peterson. "It boils, and no fire needed. But—I dunno. The heat that starts you fighting, it makes you lose the fight. There's Parrish and

79

Valdez, smelling trouble, licking their chops and ready for it, thinking about each other, sitting like two cats beside a rathole. And one day along comes a snake and swallows one of those cats."

"What you mean by that?" asked Alec.

"Aw, nothing, maybe," said the cook.

"He don't mean nothing," said Latour. "He's only a half-tide rock awash. But where's the Finn? Ukko, why don't you give us a wind?"

Birger Ukko grunted, lighting his pipe.

In Culver's mind was still the story of Valdez coming out of the sea; and the death of Parrish. He had a feeling there was something of immense power about Valdez. That was why the men never had talked about him.

The O'Doul said: "Ukko! Hey, Ukko! Give us a wind, will you? We're falling behind. Valdez is getting the lead of us. He's walking away from us."

A new light began to stream across the ship, painting the idle sails white and black in long streaks. Culver, turning, saw a golden moon rising out of the horizon mist. It was the only element of motion in the scene—the moon and the trembling of the stars.

Birger Ukko was saying: "How I give? My hand is empty. There's no weather in it."

"But what's the matter, Ukko? Why are we stuck here?" asked George Green.

"Maybe the *Spindrift*, she smell trouble," said Ukko. "Like a horse that won't cross bridge."

"What kind of trouble would she be smelling, Ukko?"

"Something dead, you think? Maybe?" said Birger Ukko.

Alec broke out: "Stop asking Birger. You oughta know that a Finn can't think of nothing but bad luck lying ahead. Now he's promised us a dead man before we sight land. Shut up and stop asking him, or he'll tell us something more."

They had been overheard by authority, as they talked. The voice of Burke came bawling forward from the poop: "Masthead Birger Ukko to look us up a wind!"

CHAPTER 12

That knocked the legend of the Nantucket sleigh ride and the death of Captain Parrish on the head and brought the idle talking to a stop. In the moonlight the men looked at one another with strange faces. Mastheading a man was, Culver understood, some sort of punishment; but he could not conceive of such a grotesquerie as putting the Finn up there at a masthead, that spear point trembling in the sky, for the sake of whistling up a wind.

A faint murmur passed among the others as Birger Ukko went aft. He stood under the break of the poop, saying: "Ay-ay, sir. But what's the use? I ain't a signal flag to raise the wind!"

"Bosun!" thundered Burke from the poop. "Masthead Ukko to look us up a breeze!"

"He's drunk," whispered Alec.

Big Jemmison began to laugh. He liked trouble in any form, particularly when it meant the infliction of pain.

"Up there with you, Ukko!" he commanded. "Lay aloft and freeze yourself onto the main masthead."

"What's the use, sir?" said Ukko.

A faint chill of excitement struck through Culver as he realized that the impossible was happening: a sailor before the mast was questioning an order. And the quiet, drawling, foreign voice of Ukko had a suggestion of patient resistance in it that would endure a deal of stress and storm.

"You heard me, Ukko. Jump!" roared the bosun. He picked up a rope's-end.

Birger Ukko still was facing the poop where Burke stood, and where the slender silhouette of the girl passed back and forth against the stars.

Ukko said, in the same patient voice: "I'm forty year at sea. Ukko never call up a wind."

"Will you jump, you lousy son of torment?" shouted Jemmison.

"By God, I'll find out if I have to give orders twice on this ship!" cried Burke. "Catching hell from the weather ain't enough—I gotta catch hell from my own crew, too! I gotta take lip and back talk from 'em, do I? . . . Now, trice him up and give him two dozen lashes. . . . I'm gonna give you something to think about. I'm gonna make you think you're back in the old days of sail, when there wasn't any sea lawyers! Trice him up, Jemmison! Two dozen, and then we'll see how he talks!"

Jemmison with his big hands stripped Ukko to the waist with a gesture. . . . The Finn submitted dully, clinging to his one phrase: "Ukko can't raise wind."

Jemmison secured him to the rigging by the wrists. He got out a cat-o'-nine-tails. No ship but the *Spindrift*, surely, would have had such a weapon in her list of equipment and stores. Someone had brought a flaring lantern. It did not help the moonlight, but threw a stain of red over the scene, like a thin wash of blood.

"Give him a last chance!" called Burke.

The sailors had followed aft. Some of them were enjoying this prospect with smirking faces. Some were agape.

Culver looked away, sick at heart, as he saw Jemmison draw the lashes through his left hand tenderly, as though he loved them. And he saw above the break of the poop the noble figure of Napico at watch, as though he would see with pleasure this degeneration of humans.

Jemmison responded to the last proffer of Burke by bawling at Ukko's ear: "You gonna lay aloft to the masthead, you?"

Ukko droned: "Ukko can't raise wind!"

"All right. He's had his chance," said Jemmison. He stood back, and Culver saw him ready for the stroke, passing the tip of his tongue over his lips, gathering himself to make the first blow a telling effort. A soft, husky, musical voice sounded on the poop. That was Koba, laughing with pleasure, showing her fine teeth to the moon. Her hero, Jemmison, was about to get into action, and she liked the prospect and the picture. Someone else came out on the poop, in time for the flogging. That was the plump figure of Jimmy Jones, that nondescript companion of Valdez who, so men said, never had left the deck of the *Spindrift* for ten years or more. It was whispered also that he rarely went ashore, because he was afraid of what the law might do to him, having broken most of the laws of most of the nations in the world, at one time or other. It was said that his unsavory intelligence formed one half of the mind of Valdez, the slimier half. He went through the world—or rather sailed through it now—with a perpetual smile of good nature. The reason for his kind expression was that he bore no malice toward his victims. A saying attributed to him was: "What dish is more succulent than a well-trimmed and cleaned sucker, nicely browned in oil? Or what is more delicious to think of afterward?" He now joined the group on the poop.

The bosun, after taking a step back, started to swing the cat-o'-nine-tails, but did not finish the stroke. A voice shouted at him: "Stop it, Jemmison! You can't do that! Good God, how can Ukko raise a wind for this ship?"

The throat of Culver ached. He realized that the voice

83

had come shouting from his own lips. And he was out there half a dozen steps beyond the others. Somehow Burke was only a black figure to him. It was Koba's face that he saw, her mouth agape in bewilderment.

"What the hell is this?" called Burke. "A half-baked mutiny, or what? Knock that damned fool down and throw him on his head in the forecastle, bosun!"

Big Jemmison turned; and seeing Culver, he laughed a little with happy surprise. In all his brutalities he had a faculty of maintaining a childish expression of innocent merriment. The business of the whip undoubtedly had appealed to him, but physical contact was still more to his taste. He stuck out his chin and rushed for Culver. A babbling of voices began among the sailors. A fight was a fight, for them. Will Carman's voice sounded off above the rest, as he called: "Kick the yella so-and-so into the sea, bosun!"

Culver heard that. What he saw was the row of black silhouettes above the break of the poop, with only Koba's face white, because in her happy excitement she had tilted up her chin toward the moon. Then he got his hands up and pitched his weight a bit forward in the boxing stance. That was automatic, with the years of shadowboxing behind it. The bosun came in with his right poised and raised like a javelin thrower about to make his cast; and when he threw his fist, Culver reached out and caught the blow in the palm of his hand while it was still two feet away.

The bosun tried to check his rush, with the result that he floundered sidewise like a crab. He was open to the head. He was open to the heart and wind. But Culver did not strike. If he hit the bosun, he was afraid that there would be malice in the blow, and he could not think of himself giving pain and taking pleasure in it; that was for the dumb beasts, not for the thinking men.

The bosun whirled around. "Missed!" yelled the penetrating voice of Will Carmen. "Now smash him down, Jemmison! Smash him!"

"Smash him!" echoed Koba's voice.

The bosum smashed with a hearty good will. He smashed with the good right hand so hard that the lurching force of the punch pulled his body around, and then he smashed with the left to straighten himself, and he waded straight in with left and rights alternately until Culver ducked in under a swinging arm and came up behind Jemmison, while the bosun was punching furiously at the rim of the moon.

The crew of the *Spindrift* had walked for a long time in terror of Jemmison. It had taken them some time to make sure that the bosun was only murdering the air, but now they began to laugh. They were laughing, but Koba was not. She was dancing in a fury on the poop, and shaking both her fists and shouting advice; but in her excitement she forgot to speak English.

Culver was breathing easily. He was hardly thinking about the bosun, but he was lost in gratitude and wonder because he was seeing every movement of Jemmison's hands as though they were caught by a slow moving-picture camera. There was little or no blur. Those overstrained eyes had been rested at last, and were taking in every detail without effort.

The bosun, turning about again, yelled out: "What in hell is this? A game of tag?" And he flung himself spread-eagle at Culver, to clutch him and bring him down by sheer weight. Culver took an inside hold. It was a heaving panting barrel that he grasped. It might have been stoutest oak at one time, that huge keg of a torso, but now is was overladen with fat. Culver did not go down. He stood against the impact with ease, and heard the bosun gasp: "But—by God—"

Then a blow struck Culver under the groin. The bosun

85

had used his knee.

Out of the yelling voices, that of Will Carman still sang above the rest: "Dirty! Hai, damn' dirty! Fight fair, Jemmison!"

The thing to do, Culver knew, was to relax, let all his body go and crumple on the deck, surrendering to that electric agony. But when he looked down, he saw the big boots of Jemmison and thought of them bashing into his face if he dropped; for the bosun was beyond himself with astonished rage; and anger, in that strange face, looked like frantic fear. Culver held himself upright. The big belly muscles were pulling like ropes to bring him down. His knees bent. He wanted to wind his arms around his body, but he had to lift them and hold them high on guard.

Jemmison twisted up his face in a final effort. He showed his teeth to the molars, and then launched another blow like an avalanche, as easy to see in its start, as easy to watch on its way. Culver ducked back. The breast of Jemmison, lunging on after the punch, struck him and knocked him to a stagger.

"Hit him, you fool!" yelled Will Carman, over the shouting. "Hit him, Culver! Tear his rotten head off, will you?"

Culver swayed over to one side. Somehow the pain seemed to warp his body in that way. He bent over crookedly and kept lifting one knee; but he managed to get one good breath down deep into his lungs.

Jemmison came in once more, like a javelin thrower again. Culver used the weight of that rush to help his own striking arm. There was plenty of time. There was half a second for drawing the bead, so he picked out the point of Jemmison's chin and banged home his fist. Jemmison's head disappeared. It came up again wabbling. All of Jemmison was wabbling, down to his knees and his shambling feet. He retreated, gasping: "My God, what's happened?

My God, how'd he hit me?"

Culver followed with limping, shortened steps. The pain still was twisting him. It had hold of all his nerves and wrung them in one burning handful. Jemmison struck out, but he struck short because he was afraid. He did not know what had happened to him before; and he certainly did not know what followed, as Culver hit again inside that reaching arm, and again his counter thudded against the jaw—solidly, with a jarring force that Culver felt up to his shoulder. Jemmison hit the rail with a crash. He had both arms stretched out against it to support his weight. There was no more fight in him, and Culver did not follow in for a flooring blow. He said: "I'm sorry, bosun!"

"Damn you!" breathed out Jemmison, and struck him down with a marlinspike which he had plucked out from the rail.

He would have brained Culver with the stroke, except for a quickly upflung arm.

CHAPTER 13

Culver was not completely unconscious. The sense which remained most alive was that of hearing, so that he made out the voice of Burke yelling: "Put down Birger Ukko and seize up Culver. Seize him up. I'll 'tend to him myself. Get his shirt off!"

And then Culver came back to his full wits with his wrists lashed into the shrouds well above his head, and the sound of the nine-tails whishing in the air, and the drawing stroke of them across his naked back.

Someone began to scream. That would be Koba. Maybe she wanted to do the flogging with her own hands. Burke panted and cursed at his labor, wielding the lash. Culver looked up at the stars that gaze on this little world and never change their faces, as though they stared but did not see us. Like a club and a cutting blade at once, the whip fell again. Culver locked his jaws together; he was silent. But the strokes of agony knocked at his throat like hands against a door that must be opened, and let the screaming out.

He tried to keep his head straightforward, but the muscles of their own volition took hold on his head and turned it so that he seemed to be looking over his shoulder to watch Burke at work. In that way, also, he was forced to see the crew in the moonlight.

He was amazed as he looked at them, for they were not watching his shame. They had turned their backs and were trooping gradually forward. Only Birger Ukko remained over there by the rail, painted black and white by moon and shadow. Birger, naked to the waist, calmly watched. It was less strange that the rest of the crew should turn their backs, thought Culver, than that Birger Ukko, for whom in a sense he was undergoing this torment, should be standing there to watch.

He began to count the lashes. He counted twenty. There had been many before. He forgot all about books and the lessons of the great. All he could do was to pray that he might faint before he screamed for mercy. He prayed that he might faint. He was willing to die rather than scream out. Unconsciousness was promised to him by waves of black numbness that rushed up from the base of his neck and entered his brain; but the next whip stroke brought him back to burning life. He could feel something running, not on his excoriated back, but down his trouser legs. That would be his own blood.

He was thinking of that when the voice in his throat escaped from him unaware.

"Oh—Christ!" his voice sobbed.

Burke shouted, completely out of breath: "Christ never went to sea. Don't call on Him. Don't pray to Christ. . . . Pray to Burke!"

The knees of Culver surprised him by giving way. He was quite in his senses, but his knees suddenly gave way and left him hanging by his arms. Perhaps Burke thought he had fainted, for the skipper panted, addressing the whole crew:

"Take this thing forward. Masthead Birger Ukko. I've been the baby of the house, on this ship. I've been a woolly little mascot for the *Spindrift*. I've been the errand boy and the playmate, is what I've been. I've been a lamb. But that's not good enough for you. Salt meat is what you want; and by God, you're going to get it. You're going to get more salt than meat. More salt than meat from now on, d'you hear? I'll teach you to like it! I'll make you like it! In the *Spindrift*, you'll know that there's either hell on board or else a wind. . . . Masthead Ukko!" He threw down the lash.

The big bosun cut down Culver.

"I can walk. I'm all right," Culver protested.

But he wasn't all right. His knees wouldn't work, and his feet dragged. The bosun took him under the armpits and helped him strongly forward toward the forecastle.

"Hell, I'm gonna get blood all over me," said the bosun, in disgust.

He got Culver forward. Other hands, a forest of them, reached up and got Culver and put him in his bunk, face down.

The bosun, panting from this work, paused to break into a strange vein of humor. "Look at what he done to me!"

he said. "Where'd he get the hammer that he had up his sleeve? Look at how he raised lumps on my chin! Whoever thought that he'd turn out to be such a ringtailed hellion as all this?"

The voice of Constantine, the Greek, said softly: "Perhaps you better go on deck, bosun."

"For why should I go on deck, you dago louse?" asked the bosun cheerfully.

"Go on deck," said Constantine, "before I cut the guts out of you. Look—with this knife!"

The bosun cursed, gasped and fled.

The forecastle was airless, thick with heat. The lantern flame was a sickening blue; there was a highlight on the sweating windlass.

"Would you like I should rub some grease on you?" asked Constantine.

Culver could not answer. There was a whisper on his lips and words coming in the hushing of that sound; he did not know what the words were, but they kept coming. He was afraid, if he unlocked his jaws, that he would begin sobbing aloud. He wanted a drink, but he dared not speak to ask for it.

He recognized the words that were whispering from his lips:

Amphi dè 'údor psuchron keládei di'
úsdon malinon, aithussoménon dè phúllon
koma katarrei.
(Around about the cool water gurgles through apple boughs, and a slumber streams from trembling leaves.)

The words became clear. The meaning became clear. The subconscious mind in him had been asking for sleep, or death like sleep. He had cried out in the agony; he had not been man enough to endure. And he wished for death as for

90

something cool and endlessly delightful.

"Udor" could not be the missing word, he was sure. "Air" would be nearer than water; air, passing through the apple boughs like gurgling water, and slumber streaming down from trembling leaves.

He made these mental annotations as he lay there on his stomach with his face turned to the side and agony turning dim the picture of the forecastle. And then he wondered at himself and at the ways of the mind, that it could take up such considerations in the midst of torment.

He thought of other things also. He thought of Burke and that murdering passion, grunting with effort as he grew tired of arm and yet continued to swing the humming cat-o'-nine-tails. One thing turned Culver sick with a sensation like that of fear; it was the memory of the weight of the whip strokes. Such power had gone into the last that it had kept knocking the breath out of his body, and it had been always impossible to breath deeply.

If it had been possible to breathe deeply, his strength of will would have remained in him, and he would not have had to groan aloud. Or if it had been day instead of night, all would have been well, he thought. He could have endured with the kind, friendly warmth of the sun looking down on him; but the cold moonlight stole away the heat of his blood and made everything mysterious. That was why the men in the forecastle were surely despising him. Constantine the Greek had made a kind of offer to rub the raw fire of his back with grease; but the rest certainly were despising him. Little Sibu, from Borneo, came and leaned above him, and made a rapid clucking sound. He knew that the clucking sound was the laughter of Sibu.

He wondered why his throat ached and burned as though he had been talking to a great throng for many hours. He wanted to take a good deep breath, but he knew that if he unlocked his teeth, he would groan loudly. That hardly mattered, because they had heard him cry out under the lash. He was strait-jacketed in fire and torment. Now the locking of his jaws was stifling him. His heart swelled and raced, and he thought it would burst. It was not blood that lay on his back, but a rank acid that was eating through his flesh into the vitals.

The harsh voice of Latour, who had no kindness for God nor man, snarled: "Sibu, what are you laughing at? What are you laughing at, you yellow dog?"

"At us," said Sibu. "I laugh at us. Pretty soon we have the whip on our backs, and not for beating that bosun."

"Stop laughing anyway, you swine," said Alec. "My God, when he was dancing around, I thought Jemmison never would lay a hand on him; and after Jemmison fouled him, I thought he'd die on his feet; and then when he started hitting out, it was gunshots through Jemmison's brain. Them hands of his went right straight through."

It came vaguely home to big Culver that they were not despising him. In fact, this seemed to be the tune of admiration. He could not believe it. He closed his eyes hard and tried to think the thing out. They had heard him cry out, surely; and yet they seemed now to have forgiven the shame he put upon all humanity. They seemed to forgive and love him for the things he had done. He felt the vast unreality of this. He had been laughed at and despised all his life.

"Ah hai!" said Francolini. "Look, look! Here it comes! Look at it!"

Someone else came into the forecastle. The tepid air seemed to grow cooler, and a fragrance mingled with the acrid scent of the rusting iron. Then he saw the gesture of a hand beside him. He could not see more than the hand, because most of his vision was obscured by the edge of the bunk and the position of his head. It was a slim brown hand.

"Get out!" exclaimed the voice of Koba. "Get out and leave him alone. In a whole ship—one man! And you make the air stinking so he can't breathe. Get out!"

Francolini said: "The bosun ain't the biggest now. The bosun's down, and there's another up."

"Damn you, dago stinkfish!" cried Koba, and jerked up her hand as though there were a knife in it. That gesture sent them spilling through the doorway. She went over and propped the door wide. It let in the air. It let in the sound of voices on the deck and trampling of feet.

Koba came back beside him. She pulled out a sea chest and sat on it.

"Now you see me better, eh?" asked Koba. "It'll make you feel better, seeing me. It is good for eyes to look at me, no?"

He tried to speak. But all he did was get a big breath high up in his chest. The air stayed there, puffing out his breast, half choking him.

"So, so, so!" said Koba.

She opened a can of stuff that let an oily perfume pass into the air, and this she commenced to rub on his back. Her touch was lighter than air. Whole sections and acreages of pain disappeared as she worked.

She paused for a moment, and leaning, took him by the short of his hair and shook his head a little.

"Make a good big noise and then you can breathe easier," she said. "Being so much man is what kills white people. It chokes them. Make a noise like a sick baby, and then you'll be stronger."

She shook him by the short of the hair; and Culver, parting his teeth for a breath, groaned long and deeply.

"Ah! Ah-ha!" said Koba. "How does that taste? Pretty good in the throat, maybe? Now try again. Make more

93

noise and get more air. So—so—so!"

Dazedly he obeyed her, and as the air breathed out from his lungs, he groaned deeply again.

"Much better," commented Koba.

"Better. Thank you, Koba; you are—"

"Shut up, fool," said Koba cheerfully. "I could make even sick fish well, very quick. Don't talk. I talk."

Her hand continued rubbing in the ointment, steadily, lightly. There still was incredible pain, but it lessened mightily from moment to moment. He tried to think of gentleness in her face; but all he could see, while his eyes were closed, was that picture of her showing her teeth to the moon.

She began a small monologue.

"I take away the pain quick. I do everything quick. I learn him English one month, and ever after speak him fine. Like you hear me."

It was impossible to repeat all the mispronunciations of Koba in the mind. The *th* for her was *s,* and all the *i's* were *e's,* all the short ones, at least.

"You speak beautifully, Koba," said Culver.

"Shut up," said Koba. "You keep your wind in your own sail, or Koba give you one hell of a whack. I talk."

She made a pause, still rubbing gently, steadily.

"How you like to see me?" she asked. "Close or far away? Close, I smell very good. Far away, you see me better. I stay far away. But I smell terrible good. My mother's-mother's-mother's grandmother make this good smell, and every morning I rub some on my forehead. Smell and see!"

She leaned her brow close to his face. The queer perfume which he had noticed before became stronger. It was almost offensive when it was so near.

"Tonight I rub on before Koba comes to you. Everybody

94

loves Koba when he smells her like this—no?" She went on.
"Now I sing. I sing best in the whole island. Everybody loves
Koba when she sings. All the old men wake up at night
when they hear Koba sing, and they stay awake till the
morning comes."

She laughed and laughed again, and once more broke
out laughing as the pleasant thought kept returning.

Then she sang, her voice breaking into a whining wail,
dying to a rhythmical murmur, whining and wailing again.

When she was silent, still rubbing the sleek of the ointment over his back, she said: "You know what he means?
It goes like this:

> The breast of a bird, how soft;
> Breast of a cloud, softer and softer;
> But softest is the breast of night.
>
> Long night, soft night, long, long night;
> And two breathing together;
> In the breast of night two breathing.
>
> Now the morning stands on the hill;
> Now the morning lies on the water.
> It is still. It is waiting. It is still.

Singing the song in the translation, she softened her voice
until there was nothing but husky music in it.

"Pretty fine, eh?" said Koba.

"Very fine," murmured Culver.

"Shut up, Culver!" she commanded. "When Koba sings,
the whole island loves her. Brown love. Not white love. Bah!
White love is a pig. It gets fat. It lies in the sun on its back
and snores. But brown love—brown love—"

She sang again in that softened voice:

> Like the sunlight under the water,
> Like the sunlight through the wave-shadows,

95

Sunlight through the blue ocean,
Sunlight on the warm ocean sands,
So is he at the door of his house,
So is he in the darkening hut,
My love, my love, my love.

"You hear me, Culver? That is brown love. Not white. Faugh. Not white love, but brown love. . . . Now go to sleep!"

His pain was so slight, now, that he almost smiled at the thought of sleep. She began to run her fingers through his hair. With the flat of two knuckles, she kneaded the base of his skull gently.

"So sleepy—so sleep!" said Koba. "Sleepy white pig, so sleep, sleep. I take all the sorrow. All the sorrow out of your body. My hands are hot with him. My arms ache with his sorrow. All his sorrow is gone away. All his sorrow is gone away into my heart. All his sorrow gone. White sleepy pig, sleep, sleep—"

Culver slept. He dropped into it as though from wave to wave, softly deeply into unconsciousness. . . . A sudden thundering of feet over his head wakened him. He heard voices shouting. The ship beneath him had a careening motion. The waves, roused out of that long silent sea, were beating rapidly against the bows.

Someone came rushing in.

"Wind?" asked Culver.

Koba was gone. There was only the highlight on the rusting iron and the smoking flare of the lantern in the forecastle. He could not make out the identity of the bent figure which was rooting around among some dunnage.

"Wind! Ay, wind! Birger Ukko has looked us up a wind!"

CHAPTER 14

When Culver's watch was called, he was soundly asleep again. He got up and turned out with the others. There was a good wind over the weather quarter, and the *Spindrift* was logging along merrily with every sail set up to the royals. He listened to the symphony of sounds. He could recognize the deep, bass-viol, soft humming of the larger rigging and the thinner violin strains of the smaller ropes; there was the rush of the sea over the side, and the rush of the wind past his ears; there was the pounding of the waves, the odd swishing noise as the ship lifted and the water seemed to be left behind; and there were dripping noises; and from the braced yards, creakings, and from the bending masts, groans, and out of the body of the ship itself indescribable deep murmurings which ran fore and aft as the living body of the old *Spindrift* gave to the force of wind and sea. He listened and he rejoiced in the noises as he identified them.

He took his place at the pump. The movement split apart the healing, crusting flesh of his back and gave him fiercer strokes of pain than the whip in the hands of Burke.

"Lay below," said Alec. "Go on and lay below, big boy. You been big enough for one day. We're all thinkin' about you. You go and lay below and don't be a damn' fool."

Culver did not lay below. He remained there at the work, swaying the weight of his body generously into it. The pain did not endure. The full bite and burn of it diminished suddenly as he looked aft and saw the skipper at his conning station on the poop. He could see the helmsman, too—and sometimes, against the stars, he could observe the man braced and striving to hold the wheel steady, as it tried to kick a spoke this way or that, obedient to the waves. But it was Burke whom he watched so intently that he was forgetting his pain.

For a new emotion had been born in him. He considered it curiously, student that he was. It gave him a cold, bright feeling inside. He felt strong with it, and his body seemed light, and yet it was a new sort of torment, too spiritual to permit his body to have much sensation either good or bad. In his hands there was a desire to close on something yielding, and he knew in spite of himself that what he wanted inside the clutch of his fingers was the throat of Burke.

He was deeply shocked. Such an emotion never had entered him before. The presence of it forced him to reconsider himself from the first to last, for he had thought that he knew Samuel Pennington Culver, and now he realized that there was in him an undiscovered country as wide and as dark as this ocean over which the ship sailed.

A seaway was kicking up. The *Spindrift* did not float over it but clove through the lifting waters. They took on some good seas. The channel ports kept clanking this side and that as she rolled. The rush of the water down the bulwarks sometimes made it seem that the lip of the ocean was hooked over the side of the old ship and that they were being buried in a weight of speeding water. It was the strongest wind that they could use royals with, he knew.

And again his mind went back to Burke. The man was big, strong, brave. He cracked on sail fearlessly and held onto it in spite of the devil and the age of his craft. The very fact that he was taking the out-trail of Valdez was probably the finest tribute to his courage, judging by the weighty silence with which the crew treated the owner of the ship. A man they would not even curse was too dark a danger to be played with, but Burke was running out across the Pacific in the hope of finding his traces.

Big, brave, patient—that was Burke; but cruel, cunning with the craft of an animal, not the wisdom of a man. With his whip he had made a dog out of Culver, and Culver felt that he never would be himself, never his own man again, until he had exacted some just and equal payment from the body of the skipper.

He was standing by the weather rail, braced to the heel of the deck, when he heard Burke's voice bawling: "Come back here, Koba, you devil!"

Then Culver saw her coming right on down the deck. The moon showed her bare feet. They left narrow tracks on the wet deck. When she reached Culver, she stood quietly beside him holding to a rope. Burke's voice followed her, then broke off into curses. She began to laugh. Holding to the rope, she swung in close to Culver so that he was looking forward and she aft.

"How is your back?" she called. "Does he hurt?"

She had her voice pitched up the scale so that the sound came small and shrill but clear to him. Evidently she was accustomed to talking through the wind.

"The back is all right," said Culver.

Francolini went by grinning to himself; and yet Culver knew that the smile was for him and for the girl, standing there together. Koba looked after him, and laughed, and nodded.

"He knows," she said, and looked up to Culver for confirmation. Culver stared helplessly forward. The moon was halfway down the eastern arc of the sky with huge, shattered clouds washing across it. The girl glanced over her shoulder and then nodded at Culver again in agreement.

"I see," she said. "Koba is like the moon, eh?"

He said nothing. She went on developing her own thought.

"Koba is shining in your mind, eh? Like the moon? The

moon is pretty good; Koba is pretty good, eh?"

She laughed, overcome by the joy of the idea.

"You think like that, eh? Oh, but you don't know. You don't know Koba. Some day he'll shine out for you. Sometime Koba, he'll make a hell of a big light for you."

She began to study his face and kept on reading it like the page of a book, from the top down. Then she turned the page, as it were, and began at the top.

"You talk pretty good. Not much. But big."

She put her hand on his arm high up, just under the point of the shoulder where the muscles are always firm.

"You are much man," she said. "You are the most man. You are for brown love; white love is for pigs. You bet the damn' life."

"I'm old," said Culver.

She took hold of him and drew herself closer, turning her ear. The wind whipped the hair away from the nape of her neck and bared her shoulder. Something went through Culver like sweet lightning through the sky.

"I'm old!" he shouted again. "Koba's young; I'm old."

She let the rope swing away and held onto Culver with both hands, laughing.

"Brown love is old, too," she said.

Suddenly he felt that he was being held by more than her hands. That single mind of his had divided into two portions. One part was holding out arms to her; the other fought against a strange sense of disaster and loss. One part of his mind saw her as she would be half a dozen years hence, her body softened with loose flesh and her face swollen; the other part of him saw her only as she was and made an eternity out of the moment.

The *Spindrift* met a rising sea, a sea that ranged aft in bright hills, polished by the moon, clipped into shining facets and fingermarked with white. And as it thumped the

100

forefoot the bell clanged, forward, clearly, with the proper touch of sharpness. Yet the hour was far from one bell.

"What's that?" shouted Burke. "What woolen head is fooling with the forward bell?"

"Him that struck that bell is lonely and wants company," yelled Peterson.

"What's that?" challenged Burke. "Who's forward that wants company?"

"Not forward," said the cook. "He's as deep as hell and aches for company. Ukko Birger said it. Somebody on board us is dying; and there's the bell calling for him."

"Hark to that bally talk!" bawled Burke. "There's more talking woman in all of you than good sailoring. You'd like to have a shark's tail on the bowsprit. You'd like to keep a damn' dove in the rigging. You're the kind that sees lousy mermaids in the white of the seafoam. There's no bad luck aboard the *Spindrift,* I'm telling you, except spitting to windward or slanging your skipper."

"On deck there!" shouted the lookout.

"Hai, hai! Trouble!" said Koba, and forgot Culver in a newer excitement.

"On deck there!" yelled the lookout. "A cloud is making out of the west, a cloud or a flying devil; no squall ever come so fast."

It came pouring out of the west, a cloud that exploded outward across the sky. Leaden-colored, curling upward in greasy smoke and its forehead overhung with knots like clustering grapes, the great bank of darkness rolled at them. The wind failed at the same moment. The *Spindrift,* which had been so full of voices, was now a silent chorus. But there was other sound, overtaking them across the sea. For now the storm head flew its tangled hair in the zenith, its forehead checked and patterned by working veins of lightning.

101

Culver was in the rigging now, driven with all the crew by shouts of the skipper. They worked with desperate hands to furl and get the gaskets on the upper canvas, and chain it down, and marl it to the yards. They worked to lash and to double-lash the main-deck boats and those amidships. And the wind began to breathe on them as it came, swaying the ship to starboard as the frightened sailors yelled and slipped upon the footropes. The darkness came. It was built high in the upper heavens; now it toppled in walls and pinnacles that burst in falling and overlaid the sky with smoky twilight. The lightning stepped between the two horizons and under it, like an outstretched shadow of the brighter flares, a phosphorescent light more softly fingered the sea. Electric fluid ran on the spars and rope-work, as the light of dawn pours a delicate fire along the dewy cables, the woven sails and infinite rigging of spiderwebs that bind together three tall blades of grass in a meadow; so the watery lightning glowed on the cordage of the *Spindrift*.

It seemed to Culver, even as he worked in touching distance of the subtle fire, that the whole image of the ship was removed and set off from him so that he saw it from a distance, like a fragile mist on a mirror's face, extenuate as thought, and thought's creation—so that the *Spindrift* and all her cargo of tinned goods and cloth and all her freighting of human lives, and all her history of many ports and many storms, her narrow pinches in the Sundra Straits, her glimpses of Cape Stiff, the Southern ice, the Northern twilight, and all the love and labor of hands that made her, might be rubbed away, might perish like words from paper, or paper touched by flame. On the yardarms and high on the trucks the corposants were flaming, and the *Spindrift* seemed to burn on the sea like a great candelabrum.

It was not a squall the eye could look through. It was as thick and solid as a city of blackness, blocks and towers and ruined upheapings of blackness. It was nothing they could luff to and spill the wind out of the sails, while a wise skipper conned her through the pinch.

They strangled in a sudden rain that closed their nostrils like submersion under water; the skipper was a ragged outline through the dimness. Hands were better than eyes for seeing, then, except when the lightning winked. But now and then Culver could see the spars quite clearly, dimly whitened by the dashing of the rain. Then the wind came in its force and blew those heavy pencil strokes of rain to gossamer mist. The *Spindrift* lay down and on her bottom the waves went thump and crash as though she were banging on a reef. Wildly the gale, with all its violins and horns was singing, high and near.

What was the matter with Burke? He was out of his head to carry all the sail that still remained on the ship. She'd smother and go down, she'd die with it, thought Culver. And all at once he wanted life as he never had wanted it before. He thought of the ship darkly wavering down through the ocean, of flat-bodied fish swimming in and out of the ports and nosing dead bodies—and he wanted life.

The ill-stowed clew of the mainsail blew out, then, and the whole course exploded into tatters which leaped and thundered on the yard.

The *Spindrift* righted a little. She split the wave tops and leaped across the hollows; and in the westerly the storm came rushing like a herd of charging elephants, tusked with lightning. They had overwhelmed the world; they had trampled flat the continents and left them awash; there remained only this last little bubble of life to stamp out—the *Spindrift*.

Still, through that uproar, Burke's voice could be distinguished, shouting: "Get off the canvas! Fore upper-topsail first. Tail all the hands along the spilling lines."

The swarming crew, how small they seemed along the deck! A sea flung a black arm over and tossed them like corks. Culver felt not even the strength of a child in his big hands.

They scrambled back to the line, patient as ants after a disaster to the column of workers. They shouted, their voices broken by the wind: "Ho! Yo-ho! Oh, oh! She goes!" With heads fallen back they tugged against the wind. The sail was like a hollow carved in crystal stone, unyielding.

"Now heave! Oh, bust her; break it! Make it run!"

They moved it. They pulled it up. They inched it along. They belayed it.

"Now up, starbowlines! Now up and furl her. Show your guts and give her hell!"

They climbed. The wind pried open lips, filled mouths with driven rain-dust. Then on the footrope, as though upon a shuddering quicksand, they fought the white bird. But still the devil was treading on the heels of the *Spindrift,* and she fled wildly.

"Get the foresail off her!" shouted Burke. "Lay down from aloft. Lay down on the run. Port buntline and clew garnets."

The big new foresail, like a wall of stone, was rigid with wind. The blocks were jammed. The lines were twisted, and the waves like molten lead slapped the poor sailors into tumbled heaps along the lee rail; but they came again, spilling the wind out, taking hold on the weather braces, gathering the slack by inches, hitching lines and holding on for life in the blind smother when they saw the heaping shadow of another sea.

At last, now, they could furl it, with two men working to pass a gasket on the massive yard.

Culver worked there with the old cook, and he heard Peterson whining: "Let her have some clothes on! She knows how to live in a wind like this. She loves it. Does Burke think that she's a stinking barge from a French canal? It's the *Spindrift* he's muzzling, the poor fool!"

Overhead came a gun crack and a tremor: They were wounded. It was like his own flesh tearing, the way Culver felt it. The topsail tye had parted and the yard fell with a roar of breaking canvas and flogging rope. It split the topmast cap and broke the parral, dropping like a vast javelin with a ten-inch haft, iron-bound, massive, forty feet in length. It crashed on deck. The wide topgallant, that passage-maker, bellied far out, bent the mast, and parting at the head, flew down the wind.

There was that voice from Burke again: "Put up the helm! Up! Up!"

"Down!" snarled Peterson. Only Culver could hear him complain. "Down, keep it down. She'll never fall away, now. You beetle-headed driveler, you marine, you dundering, lubberly coal-barge skipper!"

The *Spindrift* raced with the wind, far over. The starboard fairleads washed in a race of foam.

"Now up, girl! Up, up!" shouted the cook. "Up, my sweet beauty!" But the *Spindrift* would not right herself.

"Helm up!" screamed Burke. "Oh, damn you, up, up!"

The two men at the wheel, half in the rushing ocean and half out of it, fought to obey the order. They did not need damning to make them fight for their lives; but the ship would not answer. Like a flat disk she blew.

The loosed the topsail halyards, but the yards clung to the bending mastheads.

Culver, always close to that wise-handed sailor, the cook, heard Peterson say: "Now they've frightened her; now she's galloping all out. She's bolting out of hand. She'll jump a cliff and smash herself and all of us at the bottom. She wants her master's hand. She wants Chinee Valdez. She knows a fool is in the saddle!"

Then, in the deadly blackness to the windward, Culver saw it lift, gathering as though it dragged the bottom of the ocean, a mighty sea that rose with streaming flags and walls that tumbled down in thunder and in smoke while it still lifted like a hill. The sailors saw that black hand lifting. A yell went out of them like the cry of the rabbit when it feels the breath of the hound on its back.

The sea rose loftier than the main yard.

Then, from his place in the rigging, holding hard, Culver looked down at one speck of human life which was left sprawling on the great slant of the deck. He had a treble flash of lightning to show him who it was. It was Koba, down there. She had been hauling on the lines with the rest of the crew, making a man of herself. Now, as she tried to get into the rigging, she fell on that slippery deck as on a hill of ice. Culver went down to her, handing himself along like a monkey among the ropes. And the black hand of the rising wave he could feel behind him; the light he saw it by was the scream of the crew, piercing his brain. He got Koba. She had hurt herself in the fall. She had banged her head on the deck or something.

He had to pick her up like a half-filled sack of grain that kept trying to spill out of his arms. There was plenty of Koba; there was a hundred and thirty pounds of her and a dozen arms and legs hanging to get in his way. He had to hold her with one arm and climb with the other. Perhaps his heart should have swelled and grown great with the thought that he was saving a life. Instead, it was pinched small by the thought that she was only an islander; to the brain and life of the world she was nothing, a name, a gesture in the dark, and yet he was risking his life for her.

He got her into the mizzen shrouds a way; then the sea struck them. It struck so hard that when it hit his feet it almost knocked them off the ratline. He put his arms right around the ropes and crushed Koba against the shrouds. That sea, at full swing and gallop, covered him knees and hips and shoulders and head at one stroke. He was holding his breath in blackness. His brain, spinning, told him that the ship was upside down. Invisible hands got hold of him and pulled. In the tension, he hardly was sure whether Koba was there or gone from him.

The wave passed, and there was the head of Koba held erect, and the eyes of Koba looking into his face as though the storm did not matter. She was silent, for once. Somehow she was able to say everything without words. The wave had gone on, but he could feel the ship settling under them, beneath the thousands of tons of water; yet in spite of that Koba laid hold on his brain and made him think of her.

Then abruptly all his consciousness returned to the *Spindrift*.

She had laid right down. Her speed was quenched. She lay flat as a stone. The waves breached over her in thunder. The moon came out; it showed spray hanging in the air like shining sails, as though the ghost of the *Spindrift* already had left her and was voyaging on.

She was hurt. The poop was stripped of weathercloth, of covering-board, and gratings. Tons of water, iron-hard with speed, had burst the cabin skylight, smashed the lazarette. The long-boat on the forehouse, once like a graceful yacht, was now a raffle, a double armful of loose boards held by the lashings; where the wheelhouse had stood, Culver saw the naked steering gear and well-oiled couplings open to the sea. There was no crew, but rags and dripping peltries caught among the rigging, and voices like the salty cry of sea birds dissolved in wind but settling into a scream: "Cut the masts!" He could hear that voice settling into a sound from a single throat over the clanging of swing-ports and the salvos of wet ropes, straining, cracking.

"Axes!" shouted Burke from the main shrouds. "Axes! Axes!"

Then old Peterson lifted his grizzled head and yelled: "No axes! Don't chop her down. Wear ship! Wear ship! The main yard, square it. Haul on the main brace. Hold by your teeth, and haul!"

The crowding thunder closed over his shout like water over the lips, but already the crew was answering, and Culver with them. He was first to reach the line and cat-footed Koba with him. Sliding and scrambling on the tilted deck they grappled with the main-brace, half in air and half in sea. They hauled, and sounded a broken chanty. The yard moved. They squared it. A sailor—it was Birger Ukko—manned the wheel.

She did not spring up suddenly. She went off little by little, still dragging her lee rail under—hevay, lifeless, stupid, the *Spindrift* that once had had the body and the feathers of a gull!

"Cut! The axes! She'll never rise!" yelled Burke.

Somehow the crew in that moment listened more to old Peterson as he shouted in answer: "Give her her chance. She's given us ours. Cut her throat and she'll die and bury you all, damn you!"

A mighty sea, a father of waves, arose beside them. Instead of beating them down into the ocean, it chose to lift them on its knees.

"God stiffen you!" shouted Peterson. "If you use the axes, God stiffen you! You half-tide barnacles, you lousy scum, it's flesh and bone you'd be cutting."

The *Spindrift* staggered, heavily beaten. But in her quarters there was strength. She had the bows for speed, with plenty of rake and a narrow entrance that let her slice to windward like a knife, trailing her wake to leeward. In spite

108

of those fine bows, she came about as sweetly as a bird on the wind. And she had, as Peterson put it, a tail to sit on when she was lifted by the head. That is to say, she was built for safety in her rump—as safe, said Peterson, as though she were at anchor. She was no damned two-year-old, Peterson would say, no lousy sprinter, all neck and middle, but cut away behind to nothing. She was a stakehorse, and the distances would never kill her, not the rough going. It was those strong quarters which served her now, together with the bracing of the mainsheet, and the lifting of that sea.

It happened all in a moment as the wind shifted a little. Suddenly she rose. She flung her masts upright while from the taut ropes the dust of the ocean was shaken. The keeling deck, glassed over with yards of ocean that was green in the light of the dawn, flung its burden into the wind, and the wind struck the sheets of water into spume. On the hard knees and belly of that lucky wave they pitched erect.

That was all. They were wet as a tidewater rock and still dripping. But presently the pumps were gushing; the storm sails were pulling them on their course. Lightning speared the morning sky from side to side, and the old *Spindrift* rose, and rose, and flew.

CHAPTER 15

Days later, Culver leaned over the wireless with the earphones clasped over his head. He had the thing pretty well in hand now. He knew the whistle, like a squeaking mouse, that announced a station near in the air. He had listened to

109

messages for some time, and his ear had quickened until he was able to take down all except the fastest; but never once did he get the *Livermore*.

It was the *Livermore,* according to Burke, that Valdez undoubtedly had taken for the South Seas, but whether the *Livermore* would go directly to Valdez' destination or stop at other ports on the way, and so be greatly delayed, Burke could not tell. The whole nature of the cruise might be altered by wireless orders after putting to sea. Burke had found that out before leaving San Francisco. To remain there and watch would simply have been to drive Valdez to another port to take another ship. It was not even sure that Valdez' ultimate destination would be one of the ports of the *Livermore's* call list. If he could get close enough, he would hire a small craft and make the intervening step, of course. Where Walter Toth might be in the South Seas, in the meantime, they could only guess within a thousand miles. That was why Burke was so desperately eager to have the wireless at work in order to pick out of the air a message to or from the *Livermore*.

The day after the storm, he called Culver aft to the poop and said: "Culver, maybe I made a mistake. Maybe I got a little out of my head, day before yesterday. I was clean crazy because we'd lost our wind, and I could see Valdez sinking hull-down on us, and sliding over the horizon and then downhill all the way home. Understand? I would of beat up my own father, I guess. And you shouldn't of hollered out to stop me from Birger Ukko. You shouldn't of done that! Am I right?"

Culver kept looking at the skipper and wondering at the poisonous bitterness he felt rise in him as he stared. He could not speak. The only conversation he could have been capable of would have been with his hands. As he listened, he found himself picking out points on the skipper's face where knuckles would have a good lodgment.

The skipper did not continue this semi-apology when he felt the eyes of Culver steadily on him. He merely said: "Go off there to the radio room—and for God's sake, use your brains on that damned machine. Get the stuff out of the air. Get the *Livermore* out of the air!"

That was why Culver was leaning over the wireless with the headphones at his ears. He knew the receiver and its dials. He knew the antenna wire, insulated from the wall with heavy porcelain knobs. The ground wire he knew, touching the iron frame of the composite old ship. The third wire introduced his supply of power from the generator, passing through a transformer which stepped the current down to a hundred and ten volts, lighting the tubes.

The sending set was on the table also; but he worked far less at that than he did at the receiving, since that was the skipper's desire. They were to listen in, not talk. Besides, reception was far harder than sending. He knew in the sending set all the important parts of the heavy-duty tuning condensers, the large coil of big wire, the small coil, grid leaks, fixed condensers, the two power tubes. Anatomizing the power transformers, resistors, toggle switch, and chokes had taken him many days, for electrical theory was very dim in his brain; but he had a working knowledge at last, and that he should have arrived at one seemed miraculous to Burke. He used to stand in the doorway and listen while Culver spelled out, letter by letter, the communications that he picked up out of the air, from a freighter here, a passenger liner there; then the broadcasting continental stations would strike in from east and west and south.

But Culver was alone on this day, with big Napico in a corner, panting because of the heat and never turning his head or his eye toward his companion. All moves toward him still had to be made slowly, for at a sudden stir of hand

111

or foot, the big fangs of Napico instantly prepared to strike. It was his snarl that warned Culver that someone else was standing in the open doorway. This time it was not the skipper, but Koba. He waved his hand nervously at her, and began to write rapidly on his reporting pad as though he were taking something out of the air. The words he wrote down meant little to him.

Koba came in. Napico greeted her with a tremendous snarl and rose to his haunches. She stood with her bare legs inches from his nose, disregarding him, and leaned on the back of Culver's chair. He grew more nervous. Since the storm, her attitude of possession had become more and more pronounced. She created in Culver a queer suspense—had become one of his major concerns, along with his quiet hatred of Burke, his fears for his library, his expectancy of a meeting, at last, with the master of the dog.

And here was Koba slipping her fingers through his hair.

"I'm busy here, Koba," he told her. "Run along, my dear. I'm very busy."

She could read, barely, only barely. Now she scanned his page on the pad and stumbled through the scribbling, saying aloud: "Sal-lee Frank-lin—Sal-lee Franklin—Sal-ly Franklin. What is a sally franklin?"

He tore the page off with a jerk, tossed it on the floor, and ground it under his heel. He rubbed the sweat off his forehead with the back of his hand.

"Run along, Koba," he repeated. "A Sally Franklin is a kind of a transformer for an alternating current."

"Alternating—transformer—sally," said Koba. "Much man!"

He was silent. He wrote again, this time in little twisting Chinese characters which really could only be hinted at with a pencil; they need a fine-hair brush for their proper execution.

112

"Say how much you love Koba?" she demanded.

"Koba, tell me where you think the *Spindrift* is going?" asked Culver.

"That skipper—that white pig!" answered Koba.

"Go ask him," said Culver.

She went to the door, looked back at him, received a casual wave of dismissal, and turned away. Glancing out the door, his eye ranged aft over the battered length of the *Spindrift*. They were still at work trying to repair the damage the storm had done to her; the scars would show but her injuries were only skin deep and the body of the bark was as sound as ever. She had showed her toughness in struggling against the sea. In Culver's mind she had become a passion. Even the brute nature of Burke realized how he loved the ship, and he was assigned to the helm for two half-shifts a day, stolen from his radio listening. At those moments he lived with a purer enthusiasm than he ever had known, and a clearer delight than he had felt even when some half-discovered clue promised, for a little time, that the old Etruscan mystery was near solution.

"She likes you. She works for you. She is like that. She is a lover," said Peterson, the cook.

Since the storm, when his impromptu orders had been the saving of them, the black man had a different place on the *Spindrift*. He still was the "doctor," but the crew treated him with a very definite respect. What he had gained, Burke in a measure had lost. The sailors could not look at the tall masts without remembering that Burke would have sacrificed them in the crisis and left the old *Spindrift* without the wings which now flew her so swiftly over the blue sea. They could not see the shine of the canvas without remembering that difference between their skipper and their cook. Another man had dropped to the bottom of the list—big Jemmison. They despised him openly with their eyes, though still his bulk was too great to be insulted in words or open gestures. The bosun, however, seemed too simple to be aware of any change. He went on his way with his usual smile, his usual bellowing voice in passing on orders.

Culver looked back from the long curve of the deck and stretched his hand back until it touched the neck of Napico. There was no warning growl, to be sure, but the neck was arched and the muscles hard. There seemed to be no relenting in Napico's attitude. It was true that he seemed to prefer a position near Culver, but there was never the slightest indication of friendliness.

The patience which Culver had learned from his years with books helped him now. Just as he had persisted in his literary problems year after year, so he persisted now day after day with the dog.

Koba returned, breathing deeply, with a rosy stain in her cheeks, and rubbing her mouth violently on the heel of her hand.

"Bah—pig, pig, pig!" said Koba.

She spat on the deck and rubbed her mouth again. Then she tossed a large square of pasteboard on Culver's table.

"There," she said. "I made him give him. Do you like, Culver?"

He could guess how she had paid for the loan of the cardboard. But he forgot her at once, he was so interested in the thing before him. For on the cardboard had been pasted a page of handwriting in ink on white paper that had been torn in a thousand small bits and then patiently assembled. It was a letter with the top strip of the page torn off, the address line being gone. The rest read:

March 11

To Captain Valdez and my mates of the *Spindrift*.
Dear Friends:

114

Well, I've got it, and it has got me. I mean, I've got the stuff. It cost me hell to keep the money after you grubstaked me. There were times when I was broke and damned hungry, but I kept that stake buttoned up inside my belt and wouldn't touch it.

I saved it for the work of getting at the old *Albatross*. I worked my way down and finally I hit port and used the cash to rent a boat and hire some divers. Then I sailed out and spent a couple of weeks before I spotted the wreck of the *Albatross*.

She was on the reef, all right, but she's slipped down to a shoulder of it, and she was too deep for easy diving. I couldn't get my men to go down more than once or twice a day. So I made a fool of myself and did nearly the whole job.

I could feel the work getting me. I was spitting blood the fifth day, but I stuck at it. I got in through the bottom of the hull, because she was turned so far over that that was the easiest way. Finally I reached the cabin before I found the stuff. I cleaned out old Captain Mullaley's private stock of pearls, and believe me, it made a fine double handful, all big ones.

Mullaley, like I told, was a regular pirate, and he spent his life and a lot of gunpowder getting that collection together. And when you see it, you'll have to agree with me that he didn't waste his time or his bullets. I know pearls, and the way I figure it, there's around six hundred thousand dollars' worth even with the market low and the pearls not as good as I think. If the market is tops, there's maybe a million.

My half would make me rich enough and you fellows could have the rest, the ones of you that chipped in to grubstake me and the captain.

But my half will never come my way. I'm laid out,

and the doctor says I'm cooked. Okay. It's been fun beating the ghost of Mullaley, anyway. He won the first trick when he cleaned me out of my little haul of shell; but I took the last trick and the pot.

There's nobody I would want to pass my share along to except maybe a niece that used to live in Baltimore ten years ago. By name of Sally (Elizabeth, really) Franklin. I heard that maybe her people have moved to San Francisco, and I wish you would look around to spot them. Sally could have my part.

I couldn't trust anybody to know about the pearls. I would have got me a cut throat. So I hid them out in the woods near here and I've got the place charted. I'll explain it to anybody that comes down. But come fast and come humping, because I'm fading out.

I hope to see you here from the *Spindrift* before I pass out west. I heard I pretty near rubbed elbows with you a few months ago just before . . . sailed bound north.

Yours truly,
Walter Toth

Culver, as he finished, looked out the open door and out to sea with a troubled mind. He could not say exactly what bothered him; but something, he felt, was wrong in the letter.

He began to read it again.

"Tell Koba how good she is," pleaded the girl.

"H-m-m!" murmured Culver.

"Aie-e-e! Aie-e-e!" shrilled Koba. "You are a white pig too!"

She went to the door and flung herself down on the deck in the full glare of the sun with her eyes closed. Presently she forgot her anger and was smiling, contented by the burning heat.

116

The eyes of Culver had returned to the bottom of the letter. It was there that the words had seemed to go wrong. He had searched too many literary documents, examining literary style, not to be aware when the language went off tune a little. He thought he found the change now, in the last paragraph:

"I hope to see you here from the *Spindrift* before I pass out west. I heard I pretty near rubbed elbows with you a few months ago just before . . . sailed bound north."

It was not quite as clearly coherent language as the rest of the letter, certainly, and now he took the cardboard into the sun to examine it bit by bit. Presently he made sure that the assembly of this portion had not been done accurately by Burke, or whoever had had the thing in hand. He could tell by the way the ink diminished. Apparently that paragraph had been written in the tiny, crowded hand, with one dip of the pen, the ink failing the nib a little toward the end. But the distribution of the dark and light ink did not correspond with the arrangement of the paragraph.

He began to reassemble the writing according to the ink, and according, also, to the frayed edges of the torn paper. They had been much handled and rubbed, which made this difficult, but at last he arrived at a new grouping which made different sense and seemed to follow the probable flow of the ink. He wrote out the new paragraph and went on deck to Burke. The wind having died down a bit, the Irishman was walking rapidly back and forth across the poop, giving himself a brisk swing-about at the end of each crossing of the deck, and always pausing a fraction of an instant to look into the eye of the wind and scowl because it would not blow more freshly. Jimmy Jones, wearing a clerical collar, sat behind the captain's walk in the shadow of a sail, his hands folded across his tidy paunch, and a contentment in his eyes.

Jimmy Jones was saying: "Perhaps you don't believe in prophecy, Captain Burke."

"I'm not the captain," said Burke, annoyedly. "Damn it, you know I'm not. Valdez is the captain of this ship."

"Ah, perhaps he is," answered Jimmy Jones, "unless the sharks have eaten him by this time. But when I see you walking up and down the poop of the old *Spindrift,* every inch a sailor, every inch a commander, I can't help calling you captain. You're worthy of being one, Captain Burke. But speaking of prophecy—"

"There ain't any such thing," said Burke. "I stick my hand in my pocket, and who is gonna tell whether I have a nickel or a quarter in my fingers?"

"May I suggest that you have neither, sir?" said Culver.

"What the devil!" exclaimed Burke. "What makes you think that?"

"Because I can see that you have made a tight fist in your pocket; and a coin inside it would be painful, perhaps," explained Culver.

Burke stared at him.

"Mr. Burke is thoroughly surprised," commented Jimmy Jones. "He thought you were one of the sheep, Culver; and now he suspects that you may be the sheep dog, or even the wolf that frightens the flock. . . . We were speaking of prophecy, in which the captain does not believe. And yet there is the direct testimony of the Good Book, Captain."

"Damn the Good Book!" said Burke. "I mean," he apologized, "the Bible is all right, but it kind of gags me, Jimmy, when I hear you talking about it."

"Well, it may be inappropriate in a certain sense," admitted Jimmy Jones with his smug little smile, "and yet it is my habit to gather wisdom where I may, even from the flowers in the field and the soil from which they grow, Captain Burke. But speaking of prophecy—"

"Birger Ukko was sour," answered Burke. "He promised us that the *Spindrift* was carrying a dead man on board because the bell struck without a hand laid on it. That was only because the wave walloped us in a funny kind of a way. But along comes the storm, and no hands lost; and there you are."

"But that isn't the end of the story, is it?" asked Jimmy Jones in his soft, genial voice. "There is still time for someone to die on the *Spindrift,* isn't there? Personally, I'm waiting with a great deal of concern. I can't help wondering who it might be. All such good fellows. All! I even feel worried a little about you, Captain."

"About me? What the hell you talking about?" demanded Burke.

He was startled and a little frightened.

"Go ahead and try to make sense out of that!" he directed.

"Well," said Jimmy Jones, "our friend Culver, here, was able to tell what you had in your hand, and so perhaps he can tell me what I have in my mind."

"Could it be Captain Valdez?" asked Culver.

The shock of this jerked Jimmy Jones off his stool and spun the skipper around in the midst of a stride.

"Valdez!" said Burke, and then he was silent, though ugly unspoken words kept his lips twitching.

Culver explained his process of mind by quoting:

> Take heed! Take heed! For though
> the king's afar,
> His shadow still is stretched across the
> land.

"Ah, Culver, you are a man of books," said Jimmy Jones. "I have been wondering what it was that gave you the air of abstraction, and now I understand—for a man of books must tag from his memory all the things that he sees with his eyes, and thought itself has no validity for the scholar unless he can wall his idea snugly in between quotation marks."

119

"So Koba brought that to you, did she?" said Burke, pointing to the card which Culver carried in his hand. "Give it to me!"

Culver proffered it. It was snatched away by an angry hand.

"Lemme tell you something about that Koba. You fool around with her, and you'll wake up some morning with an extra mouth carved under your chin. She'll cut your throat for you, Culver!"

Culver considered the remark in silence for an instant; then he said: "In regard to the letter, there: the final paragraph is put together wrong."

"Wrong? Wrong?" exclaimed Burke. He scowled at the card. "No, it makes good sense, all right, and I don't see anything wrong with it."

"I take it," said Culver, "that that paragraph is what gives you direction for this voyage. You touched at certain points in the South Seas, and you are returning to them to search the islands all around those ports."

"Maybe that's right," nodded Burke.

"It would be a long work," suggested Culver.

"Unless we have luck," admitted Burke. "And we're gonna have luck. I feel it in my bones we're gonna have luck. And I'll tell you something more, Culver: If you play the game with us and handle Napico on shore like a good fellow, we're gonna cut you in for a full share of the stuff."

Culver was silent again. It was hard to make himself talk to the skipper. But now he managed to say: "Regroup the words properly in that last paragraph, and it should read as follows: 'I hope to see you before I pass out. I pretty near rubbed elbows with you a few months ago, before I heard the *Spindrift* sailed from just west (of) here, bound north.' Those are the same words, you see, but they make better English. In the former version: 'I hope to see you here from

120

the *Spindrift'* is clumsy."

"Are the words all in?" demanded Burke. "They are! They're all in, and it does make better sense."

"The advantage," said Culver, "is that when you think over your last voyage, you perhaps can remember a port at which you touched with another island immediately to the east of it."

"Wait a mintue," said Burke, rapping his forehead with his knuckles. "Wait—Salter's Island. . . . No, that's no good. That's too north of east. . . . Wait!"

"When we touched at Wago," suggested Jimmy Jones, "Tapua was immediately to the east."

"It was! It was!" shouted Burke. "By God, I knew that there was good luck on board the *Spindrift* somewhere, and you're it, Culver! You're dead right! Oh, God, now for a bellyful of wind! Tapua is the place! Tapua! Now, Valdez, watch yourself!"

He went rushing below to find a chart, and Culver turned away to return to the radio house, for he had something else in mind that needed doing at once.

"We must have some time together, Culver," suggested Jimmy Jones.

"Yes, sir," answered Culver, without enthusiasm.

"That was very neat about the coin in the hand; but much neater about the king and his shadow across the land," said Jimmy Jones. "Would you step down with me now and have a glass of port? A glass of Valdez' own port?"

Culver followed him down the companionway and into the captain's cabin, which Burke, strange to say, did not occupy. Napico, appearing noiselessly from the deck, slipped into the cabin behind them, and trotting into the small adjoining room, jumped up on the bed and lay there with his paws dangling over the edge and his tongue lolling out as though he were laughing at these two intruders, and yet keeping strict guard over the only place of real importance.

"So long as no one sleeps in the bed of Valdez," said Jimmy Jones, "Napico seems reasonably content. That is to say, he doesn't mind the afterguard, with whom he's familiar—the second, and Burke, and Koba and me. But if one of the sailors—other than your very exceptional self, Mr. Culver—were to step into this room, Napico would go for his throat as quickly, and as accurately as—well, as a knife out of Koba's hand. . . . Did you ever see Koba throw a knife, Mr. Culver?"

"No," said Culver.

"Extraordinary child," said Jimmy Jones, opening a cupboard which was set into the dark, carved paneling of the cabin. "Beautiful and interesting." He pointed to the wall. "There is one of her few misses," he said, indicating a deep scar in the panel. "Her knife missed the throat of Valdez by a fraction of an inch, and yet somehow her intention was entirely clear. . . . To your good health and our better acquaintance, Mr. Culver."

Culver sipped the liquor. Jimmy Jones had poured down his glass and filled off another.

He said: "I like to get my tongue covered to the roots before I start trying to get the taste. A first glass for a drink; a second one for an opinion. And now that we know each other a little better, my I give you a word of advice which is for your honorable ear alone?"

"You are very kind," said Culver.

"You have observed Burke? You understand him?" suggested Jones.

Culver was silent.

"At least," said Jones, "I can say that he is a very honest fellow, since he honestly serves Burke and lets the rest of the world go hang. And no matter what you might do for him, in the end his promises to you would tie him down no more than the sheerest, the most intangible spider thread. It is obviously his purpose, when he gets ashore with his men, to use your hand on the leash which controls Napico, and let Napico hunt for sign of Valdez. In this manner he expects to use the dog to betray the master. Interesting thought, isn't it? The heart of the dog swelling with love as he strains down the trail of his friend, his man of the whole world, his adored Valdez; and with every step he takes, drawing incalculable mischief upon the head of his captain! That is the picture which Burke has in mind. If you should refuse to take part, he would find means to persuade you. You already know that he is eloquent in acts of persuasion."

The flesh crawled upon the back of big Culver as he remembered.

"Therefore I advise you," said Jimmy Jones, "to find the first opportunity ashore to give them all the slip and become your own master. If the dog then takes you to Valdez, you come as a herald giving warning that the enemy approach. And in that case, I imagine the captain would find means to give himself adequate—er—protection."

"I understand," said Culver, watching the fat little man with curious attention.

"And as for reward," said Jimmy Jones, "you have in Captain Valdez a man as generous as the sea, as open as the wind. All that he has belongs to the needs of his friends. You could trust him, Mr. Culver, to assist you to the last extreme."

Napico, in the next room, weary of lolling out his tongue as he panted, retracted it to lick his lips and gave an impatient whine.

"So, so, my beautiful Napico!" said Jimmy Jones. "You shall not be used to trail your master; you shall not be used like a knife to cut his throat. Mr. Culver will not permit it, so you may trust everything to him, Napico, my fine boy."

"You are a devoted friend of Captain Valdez, are you not?" asked Culver.

"In one word," said Jimmy Jones, "I know him; and to know Captain Valdez—to know him to the heart and to the marrow of the bones—is to love him."

"And yet," said Culver, "it seemed to me on deck, a moment ago, you were helping Burke locate the island where we are likely to find Valdez."

"Did you notice that?" asked Jimmy Jones, blinking a little. "The fact is that I know how the drama will end, but I am anxious to see the third act of the play. Here we have the honest Burke and all his men, that uncanny wizard Birger Ukko who calms the wind or makes it blow; our worthy Alec, who they say has eaten strange fish in his time; Sibu, who has made a splendid collection of heads, and only needs a few long-haired blondes to complete the set; Francolini, who is another Borgia; Latour, who is as full of devices as Odysseus; and all the rest of them, to say nothing of melancholy George Green, who has killed more men than all the rest put together. I contemplate the engine of the opposition, a grand opposition, a beautiful opposition. And I see them striking for the heart of our hero, a single man, a single hand against them all. One Captain Valdez against that whole army. And yet, of course, he is sure to win!"

"Why are you so sure?" asked Culver, who was following somewhat from a distance the intricacies of this argument.

"Doesn't the hero of a proper play always win in the end?"

"But this, it seems to me, is not a play," said Culver. "It is not a contrived play, Mr. Jones."

"Valdez will contrive to make a play of it," answered Jimmy Jones, "and that's why I cannot wait for the moment. You understand, Mr. Culver? On the one hand I detest the thought of these forces of the opposition overtaking my dear Valdez; for that reason I take you aside and advise you how to act in order to keep mischief from the head of my good friend. On the other hand, I desire nothing so much as the climax of the piece and cannot help letting Burke have a glimpse of destiny, even though it be only through a crack in the wall. I hope it is all clear to you now?"

"In the first place," said Culver, "if they overtake Valdez, they are apt to get the pearls which he is trying to keep for himself, and I dare say that you detest the thought of Captain Valdez robbing them?"

"Ah, my dear Mr. Culver," said Jimmy Jones, "do not be ironical. Irony is the weapon of the weak and the tormented. . . . Will you have another glass?"

"I thank you, no," said Culver. And excusing himself, he went back to the radio room.

CHAPTER 16

In the radio room, he leaned over his table, threw the switch engaging the receiver, then the general switch connecting the receiver with the antenna. After that he threw the power-supply and transmitter switches to give them a chance to warm up. He clasped the earphones over his head, and then manipulated the dials on the panel board for the station he wanted, the short-wave station of Tommy Wiley. He heard whistlings as he turned the dials; he heard a message clicking from a ship; he heard someone giving XVL, the call letters. Then he engaged the transmitter, and with the operating key sent out "C Q" half a dozen times. There was not much chance of getting a reply from the little sending set of Tommy Wiley. He could only hope that the condenser and coil of his invention were truly as fine as he hoped. In that case, if Tommy were at his instrument, the message had a chance in a hundred of reaching its destination. He began at once to send his words: "On board the *Spindrift* sailing for Tapua where Walter Toth is dying with large fortune waiting for you. Urge you take fastest possible passage for Tapua. Kindest regards. Samuel Culver."

He waited, listening eagerly at the receiver. Then he repeated his message once, twice, and again.

He had just thrown the switch back to the receiver for the last time when the voice of Burke boomed through the doorway: "What are you sending, Culver? Who are you trying to reach?"

"I'm practicing," said Culver.

"You've got a buzzer for practice," commented Burke. "What the hell is the meaning of this?"

"A buzzer is excellent practice, but it's not exactly like an operating key, sir," said Culver.

"I'll have no more of this damned nonsense," stated Burke. "You send when I have a message for you to send. Otherwise, keep your finger off that key!"

He disappeared, and Culver leaned back in his chair. He could not help thinking of his message as traveling still through the air on urgent winds of sound; in reality he knew that already the swift impulses were girdling the world at the rate of half a dozen times a second. Either Thomas Wiley had heard, or the message never would reach its destination, for he would not dare to use the key again. He knew, as Jimmy Jones had suggested, the means of persuasion which Burke was capable of using.

That evening the crew was wondering why the *Spindrift,* with yards braced well around, was on a new tack, heading to the southwest instead of into the southeast. The trades caught her more favorably on this point of sailing. She could

126

make steerageway, old Peterson used to say, with the flap of her sails; under the fresh, steady breeze she skimmed like a gull with all her wings stretched.

Nothing altered; nothing changed. The days went by as steadily as the wind. Culver tried to keep his imagination from seeing and reseeing Sally Franklin and young Wiley packing their bags, hurrying aboard a steamer; he tried not to see them standing forward to feel the bow wind, and watch the cutwater shearing off the bow waves on some big liner that was sliding south with a shudder of creaming sea along her black sides. Tapua was not a port of call, he learned among the crew, for ships of any size. It was only, they said, a midget of an island, a tumble of mountains and jungle with a few white strips of beach fringing it, a bit of reef to shelter the harbor from certain winds, and a scattering of huts and houses to make a village. It could be reached by a small steamer that plied to Wago now and then, they believed. When he heard this, Culver gave up the slim hope of their coming. Perhaps there would not be time even for a fast steamer to make the voyage from San Francisco before the *Spindrift* reached her destination, though altering the course added nearly a thousand miles to the journey before she touched her first harbor.

When the fresh breeze lightened, when they lay for five days with not enough logging to count against drift, his heart was lightened and he could not help looking again and again along the northern horizon in hope that he would see the smoke of an approaching ship. And then they got a fine following wind and made Tapua the next day.

The smoke from the little volcano looked like that of a steamer, at first; but as they drew nearer the source, the smoke lifted into the sky, and finally they could make out the mountain. It seemed to stand by itself, rising steep-sided from the ocean like a whale that had come up to spout and

127

would disappear into the deeps again the next moment.

Two hours before sunset of that same day, on his wireless he got the *Livermore*.

He had tuned the instrument very fine, and the *Livermore's* call came faintly but surely into his ears. He noted her position. Apparently she had finished her southern voyage, loaded, and was far up north again toward Honolulu.

He took that message, written out neatly, to the skipper. Burke turned pale as he read. He could not actually grow white; the red of his skin was too intense for that, but he altered to a sort of gray purple.

"Then Valdez—he's had weeks on us. He's had weeks on us!" said Burke. "Weeks—weeks—and it's Valdez who's had them!"

Tapua was now revealing itself more clearly with every mile made toward it. The wind was light. They crept over the sea in the late afternoon without a sound from the rigging, without a whisper from the sea. The volcano showed now a group of lesser companions crowded about it. They were near enough to see the green of foliage, and see the white streak of water near the reef before the sunset confused everything in a colorful mist. Tapua disappeared. It was seen once more in the moonlight, a picture remade and created in close detail as the *Spindrift* stole upon the scene and made itself a part of the whole. Tapua now stretched far to the right, far to the left, and the soft booming of surf on the reef made a drum note of music that struck regularly on the ear. A half moon hung down low on the sky, suspended invisibly, and poured out silver along its path on the water, a bright silver hardly tarnished by the wrinklings of waves, the ground swell was so even, so smooth of face except where it tripped its feet and tumbled on the reef. . . .

Culver was oiling a forecastle winch when Koba appeared beside him and sat down cross-legged, her back to the rail.

"You swim, Culver?" she asked.

"I used to swim well. But not for years and years, Koba," he told her.

"You swim good," stated Koba. "You have cold blood like a fish. You swim pretty good, I guess. Swim now, Culver."

"Why should I swim now?" he asked.

She flicked her thumb aft.

"Burke," she said. "He has irons to keep you till he needs Culver on shore. You swim now."

He could hardly believe what she said. He glanced over the bows toward the shore. They had seemed almost in on the harbor for a moment before, but the thought of swimming lengthened the distance as he measured it out in imaginary arm strokes, until it seemed an endless journey. Off to the right, and ahead of them, lay the reef, making its rhythmical thunder in the surf as the ground swells heaved and fell and whitened.

"Hi, Culver!" called George Green. "Lay aft to the skipper!"

Culver kicked off his shoes.

"Yeah. You swim," said the girl. "Take off his clothes and then swim better, Culver."

He did not pause to take off his clothes. He could see Burke waiting there aft, on the poop. He could see a different picture of that shore scene, now. There would be no chance to take the good advice of Jimmy Jones and give the shore party the slip, if he were taken onto the island to find the trail of Valdez. They probably would put hobbles on him and tie the leash of Napico to his wrist.

Culver said: "Koba, you've been a kind girl to me. Be careful of yourself, my dear. And good-by!"

She had her chin on her fist, and she made no answer whatever.

129

Culver stepped over the rail.

"Culver!" he heard George Green shout. "Lay aft!"

He sprang well out from the ship, forming his arms and hands into a prow above his head. The water stung his hands and bumped the back of his neck. It was not a graceful dive. He was aware of a big splash; then he was sliding down through the sea, swimming hard. He came to the surface opposite the waist of the ship. Francolini had run over to the starboard rail to watch him. Green was there. So was Birger Ukko and Sibu. They all laughed and chatted together and pointed him out. In fact, his strokes of swimming had not carried him far. The nearness of the *Spindrift* held him in a sort of charmed circle. He seemed to be making futile gestures with arms and legs to get away.

Aft, he saw Burke shaking a fist in the air, not toward the swimmer but at the world in general, and shouting orders to get a boat into the falls and lower away. Forward, there was quite another picture. Koba stood on the rail, at ease and secure as a circus performer, pulling off her dress and tossing it away behind her on the deck. The wind caught it, however, and hung it over the rail, like a bit of blue laundry. Except for the dress she had not been wearing much of anything. She bent her knees, gave her arms a swing, and then cut the air into the sea.

She disappeared. Presently a brown streak came up in the water beside him. He thought of sharks; then he saw it was Koba. She stood up out of the sea almost to the hips and gave the water a fling out of her hair.

"Culver is a slow pig in the water," she said.

Once he had read a romance in which the hero and the heroine swam ashore like this. They had come in from a life raft, and there had been writing about the hero's strong body and the heroine's slender one, and the way the water buffeted his shoulders, and the smooth way she cut through

130

the waves. There might be that sort of a picture now, but there was no romance in it for Culver. In the story the feature had been the couple treading water and giving one another a long embrace before the disaster was about to befall them. The disaster was a big wave, or something like that. Culver was irritated in remembering the thing. All he wanted right now was to get away from the *Spindrift*.

"This way!" said Koba, and cut out ahead of him. She seemed to take a stroke and sail, and wait, and look back at him. He seemed swimming in sticky liquid; she seemed floating in air. It was a queer difference.

He saw the ship was suddenly much smaller. And in a single eye-grasp he could take in all of her from the stem to the stern. He saw Napico's head and shoulders rearing above the after rail. The big dog was watching. Perhaps he would dive over and join the swimmers. Culver with his whole heart prayed that this might happen, because somehow he had had the feeling from the first that Napico was leading him somewhere.

He worked off his trousers. That left him freer for the swimming. The water seemed to slide past him more smoothly, but in the meantime he saw that the boat was swinging from the davits; it was dropping; then it was in the water.

Something roared in his ears, very close.

"Koba!" he called. "You're heading for the reef! We can't go that way."

She lifted her head and looked back at him, swimming on her side without effort. She reached out with the under arm and hauled herself far forward at every stroke. Her feet kicked just below his head. But she held on her course straight toward the reef. They were already in the larger heave of the waves as they gathered themselves for the run at the reef. Coming up to the top of a ground swell, he saw

131

clearly the lift and the crash of a comber on the coral, with weight enough to shatter a man's bones.

"Koba! Koba!" he called, but she kept straight on.

It might be that she had water in her ears and could not hear him. Or perhaps the roar from the reef, momentarily louder, drowned out his voice. He put on a strong spurt, swimming his fastest. But she, without specially increased effort, kept the same measured distance ahead of him. Already, it seemed to Culver, they were irretrievably in the swing of the waters, heading for trouble.

He reached out, at last, to catch her by the foot. His fingers touched her, but the foot kicked away and was gone like a frightened fish.

There was no taking her away from this dangerous course; and there was no leaving her, it seemed to Culver. When he looked back, he could see the boat coming off from the *Spindrift,* and in the stern sheets, standing up, laughing, was big Jemmison with a boathook in one hand, the other laid on the tiller. It would be a thought natural to Jemmison, to pull a human fish out of the sea with the steel hook which he carried! Culver, turning face down, swam on desperately behind the girl.

There is nothing like swimming to take it out of a man; the muscles of Culver, so well trained for other work, began to grow numb with this unusual movement, and the wind went out of him as though he had fallen from a height. He tried one last time to call the girl; but when he lifted his head, he saw that it was too late. The swing of a sweeping ground swell already was picking him up and driving him forward at such speed that it was enough to use his strength to keep his body straight without trying to make headway. He prepared to fend for himself with hands and feet when the reef rose under him; but he knew the thundering force of the water as the wave tumbled its crest over and dropped,

132

with the lunging shoulder sliding behind it. Koba was lifting her head, looking forward, and then smiling back at him.

He looked back, and saw the boat with its prow not ten yards away; but it hung there, growing more distant, as the crew backed water hard. The pull of the ground swell must have surprised them with the strength of its grip and the speed of its swinging motion.

Then he looked again toward Koba. The thunderous leaping of the water was right before him. Beyond it he saw the smooth water of the inner lagoon, sleeked out as though with oil, moving only in long, slow pulsations as the shattered waves reformed with the last impulse of their strength and rolled leisurely on toward the beach. The moon silvered a long path across those pleasant waves.

Beyond the lagoon there was the whole usual picture of a tropical island. There was the blanched sand of the beach rounding in a big arc at the lips of the sea; there were the tall palms with the dead skirts of a hundred years falling down around their shanks. There were the mountains with dim glimmers of fire in the open entrances. Off to the side appeared, on a highland, a house and some outbuildings which showed the presence, probably, of the usual trader.

Culver had time to smile a little as he looked at this sketch. Somehow his eyes remained set upon it, because they feared to look at that nearer picture. The roar of the breaking surf made thinking difficult now. And because his brain was befogged by the noise, he did not even try to find his own way but followed Koba blindly.

A larger wave than any of the preceding ones picked him up, lifted him high and flung him ahead. From that flying top he could see, at last, that there had been reason in Koba, after all. For the reef apparently did not run in an unbroken wall. Right ahead of the reaching arms of the girl the seas sluiced through a gap in the reef. It was not a wide opening,

and the water came pouring in from either hand and inter-
mingling in a twisting current which no swimmer could make
head against. Still, there was that gap, like a hole in a rabbit
fence, and he understood at once that she had come in this
direction because it was the only possible avenue of escape.

She was right on the lip of it now. He saw her go up on
the crest of a wave. She turned. One arm flashed as she
waved back at him. He saw her head turned also, and her
voice cut through the thunder and reached him like the small
cry of a child in the night.

Then the wave heaved on, blotting out the lagoon, the
beach, the palms, the mountains, leaving only the smoking
tip of the volcano in view above its upper ridge.

He, in the meantime, had fallen into the trough, but a moment later he was picked up as by a thousand urgent hands
and tossed toward the stars. He lurched forward. The spinning crest shot him ahead. He looked down a steep bank and
sharply descending hill of water which to the right and the
left curled over and formed its visible thunder along the reef
but just ahead of him the wave sloughed outward, suddenly,
and poured through the gap in the coral.

He had a bewildered glance ahead, but he could not see
Koba. Then the rushing current in the gap took hold of him,
fingered him, and hurled him right on and down. He tried his
best to keep his body straight. In spite of himself he was
whirling around and round. The motion eased. But he was
deep, dark fathoms beneath the surface, with pressure on his
whole body. Gradually this relaxed. He swam strongly upward toward a glimmering light, and so with bursting lungs
his head broke surface again.

He was blind with coughing and gasping for the moment.
But when at last he had winked his eyes clean, he saw Koba
in the water beside him, laughing.

"Oh, if they only had come two oar strokes closer—two

strokes more—two strokes more!" she cried out. "They would have been tumbling here like wet white pigs. Tumbling and drowning!"

Culver floated on the smooth lagoon with casual swimming strokes while he regained his wind. He could look back at the *Spindrift* beyond the white heads of the combers on the reef and see her with down-drooping sails, black and white in the moonlight. In the nearer distance, he saw the boat which had escaped the reef, oaring over the surface of the inner lagoon—moving in pulsations, like a water bug that glides on the surface. Far off, he heard the plump of the anchor, the rattle and roar of the chain. Then he saw Koba stand up out of the water. They had come unexpectedly into the shallows of the lagoon, and the beach was immediately before them.

CHAPTER 17

No doubt Culver should have been watching the dark Venus who was rising from the sea beside him. Koba herself was expecting a great effect and moved slowly, elaborately, aware that a few dragglements of wet underclothes were all that pretended to hide what God had given to her in a large-hearted moment of creation. Knee-deep in the soft sway of the lagoon waters, she paused and improved her contour by lifting her arms to wring the water from her hair, which was of a texture that fluffed out almost immediately. But Culver was more conscious of the sagging weakness in his knees and the weight of his tired body. In his mind moved a jumble of odd effects, as he entered into this new quarter of the world. He thought of Mrs. Lindley and his

135

books, of the light that had trembled in the red hair of Sally Franklin, of Napico, and again of Sally Franklin and the green in her eyes. A bit guiltily, he glanced at Koba.

"Koba, that boathook would have been ripped into me, but for you," he told her, and touched her shoulder in gratitude.

Koba instantly drew his arm around her.

"Now everything is all right," she said. "My uncle Takono is big man in Tapua. He takes one Valdez, one Burke, and bumps their heads. . . . You like Koba pretty good, Culver?"

"You're a remarkable girl," understated Culver.

" 'Remarkable? Remarkable?' " echoed Koba, squinting her eyes as she tried to get the desired taste out of the word. "There is brain in Koba. Much brain. She speaks English helluva lot, eh?"

They began walking on slowly, as though the *Spindrift* never had been in their lives, as though the tall ship were the merest incident, a part of a picture from which they were far divorced. Culver grew aware of his costume and the dripping of his shirt-tails.

"You speak a great deal of English," answered Culver. "How did you come on board the *Spindrift,* my dear?"

"Everybody is damn' fool once," answered Koba, brushing the *Spindrift* out of the conversation with a very personable gesture. "Koba was damn' fool. There is Takono's house. Very fine, eh?"

The straggling buildings which he had seen from beyond the reef had turned into a fair-sized village with a hint of streets and some European structures grouped around the foot of a long pier. The palms and the trees had covered a great part of the picture when it was seen from a distance. Now they were heading up the slope of an easy hill with a big, round-sided hut on the flattened side of it.

136

He looked back through the palms, which were drawing together more thickly behind him; he still could see the shining sails of the *Spindrift*. But now everything connected with his immediate past seemed absurd and dreamlike. The present strangeness dimmed all thoughts of the ship, the shanghaiing in San Francisco, the dim figure of Valdez. If he had been asked what he would have with him out of his entire past at that moment, he would have answered that he wanted Napico to trot on ahead of him at the end of a leash, smelling out a way, for Napico was the unsolved problem which loomed out of his past; and to win the confidence and the love of the dog seemed, for mysterious reasons, almost as important as discovering a key to the Etruscan language.

With these thoughts Culver's mind was filled as he walked through the black-and-white strips of moonlight and shadow in the palm grove. The warm, humid air touched his body like tepid water, and the scent that it carried to him was utterly new, as though a different soil gave birth to different plants.

He found himself saying: "Where is it among the poets, Koba, that there is talk of a woman and the sea? Is it somewhere in Homer, or in the legend of Aphrodite, the foamborn, that we learn to think of women and the sea? Now my mind has been traveling very far from you, to tell the truth, but all at once the wind breathes something into me, and I can think of Koba only."

"Ha-ha?" murmured Koba, half questioning and half delighted.

"Where is it among the poets," went on Culver, thinking aloud in his gentle voice, "that they speak of the danger and the loveliness and the wildness and the song of the sea, and find it like the delightful peril and the beauty and the strangeness and the voice of woman?"

"Koba?" she asked.

"As a matter of fact, I seem to be thinking suddenly of you alone," said Culver. "But where is that thought among the poets? Theocritus? No, not there. He is too slight for that. Pindar? He has sweeping images like that; but would he use such images for a woman?"

Koba began to sing as softly as the rushing sound of the trade wind through the palms. Culver was silent.

"Talk! Talk!" said Koba, and went on with her muted song.

It began to run into the mind and the thoughts of Culver like an accompaniment of the words which drifted from his lips almost unconsciously, now.

"Infinitely varied, varied most infinitely," said Culver. "Do you know how I see you, Koba?"

Instead of answering, she continued her singing, looking straight ahead, smiling to herself. An odd excitement entered Culver, but he suppressed this as well as he could.

"It is an image of a thousand parts," said Culver, continuing his thoughts aloud. "If there is pain, I remember Koba in the forecastle taking it away with the touch of her hands. That was the beginning. I think if I ever find pain again, the sort of pain that breaks the heart of a man in two, I shall remember your hands, Koba. Do you understand that?"

She continued her wordless song without an answer.

"But no matter what emotion might be in me," said Culver, exploring the idea with a growing wonder, "I think there would be a picture of you to match it. If I had an easy, slothful content in the warmth of the sun, when the heat of it like sleep relaxes the body and passes its fingers down to the deepest weariness and gives a perfect peace, I should think of Koba lying flat on her back on the deck with her arms thrown out, embracing the sun, smiling."

"Ah—ah—," murmured Koba, and continued her song again.

138

"And if I were ever tiptoe and alive with happiness, I would think of Koba swimming in the sea like a bird floating in the sky. Or if—or if—" He paused.

"Talk!" breathed Koba.

"This is hard to say, because it is quite new to me," said Culver, "but the truth is that if I ever again find a strange mournfulness in my heart, a sorrow with a happy core to it, a homesickness that persists when one is already home, and a desire to take what is already given, and a hunger in the midst of a food, a thirst in the midst of drinking, I shall think of Koba and this song of hers, like the wind, or the sound of the distant surf."

A sudden rattle of cheerful voices broke upon them through the trees.

"Ah, my God, they will end it!" whispered Koba. "Come away! Quickly, quickly—"

She pulled at him to step aside behind a huge old palm trunk; but it was impossible to hide from the crowd of islanders who swept up around them, and caught at the girl with many hands.

Culver, surprised, listened to the babbling of their tongues with curious and happy ears, for it was a language richer in quick, soft vowels than any he ever had studied in all the years of his life. But over and over again he heard the name "Koba," and saw clearly that she had fallen among friends. Men and girls, these creatures moved in a way different from people who wear shoes; there was a languor even in their swiftest gestures. They had not about them the sweaty savor of civilization but a queer pungency of odor that was half a fragrance, like the perfume of good cookery. Now they were urging both Koba and Culver forward, drawing them up the slope, laughing, shouting. And as they went, they cried out repeatedly: "Kava! Kava!"

He identified the word readily enough. An intoxicant curiously prepared in the South Seas by scraping and chewing

139

the root of the kava. The expectorated mouthfuls—the saliva having separated the alkaline from the sugar content—ferment rapidly. The juice of coconuts is added liberally. Presently a mild intoxicant is in readiness.

Now they emerged from the palms of the grove into the open before the big hut they had seen from a distance. It was apparent at once that a festival was going forward. Several fires burned in the open with big pots simmering over them, and the good odor of cooking meat and other edibles filled the air happily, for Culver. The moonlight and the light from the fires and the light from lanterns hung here and there filled the open space with a confusion of many shadows that angled out in all directions, making black, sprawling caricatures of every outline; Culver saw more bare humanity at a glance than he had dreamed of during the years of his life. It was far from a pleasant spectacle. He turned to rest his eyes on Koba, but she was gone, running to throw herself into the arms of the host.

Takono did not rise to greet her, because rising was difficult for him. He sat cross-legged on a mat in the center of things—a pyramidal edifice, squatting on his huge thighs. He was grotesque, yet there was a sort of magnificence and beauty about him. He embraced the girl and then held her for a moment like a baby in his arms, trundling her back and forth, laughing and talking to her. And around them a ring of girls danced, all with flowers adorning them. They made a lovely sight in motion; but when they were still, their beauty diminished. Even their faces seemed made more for laughter than for repose. They would have been trebly charming as a passing procession, not as a stationary show.

Koba was on her feet again now, and running to Culver, she drew him across the open circle to the fat man. Takono put out an immense moist hand that fairly swallowed the grasp of Culver. He was hugely conscious of his damp shirt-tails, by this time, but his embarrassment was not shared. The chattering Tapuans gathered about and looked at him with the greatest friendliness and a sort of anatomical curiosity that paid heed to every detail. The big thigh muscle, divided above the knee and folding loosely down beside it, particularly took them. An old man actually got to his feet and came over to poke a forefinger into that muscle. The hardness of it made him laugh with pleasure.

Koba began to sell Culver like an ox at a fair. What her rapid voice said of him he could not tell, of course, but her gestures spoke for themselves with the utmost eloquence. It was presently apparent that an almost superhuman brain resided in the head with which she endowed him; and it appeared that no matter how the wind blew, he was at home in the rigging. In the air she sketched the monstrous figure of the bosun, reaching on tiptoe to draw in the outline of his towering head; and with a blow of her hero's hand she shattered the giant to dust and gravel underfoot, and kicked it for good measure. She made the *Spindrift* lie flat in the ocean once more and with her speaking hands she built up the great wave until it overwhelmed the ship once more; and she showed herself prostrate and senseless on the deck under the shadow of the wave, and indicated her hero swinging down like a bird from the sky to seize her and bear her up to safety. She even indicated the thundering reef, and her man of men sliding through the gap in the coral into the smooth safety of the lagoon.

When she had finished, there was a loud, hearty shouting, and the aft hand of Takono drew Culver down beside him. In that seat of honor he remained as the feasting began. It was a copious meal with everything served on great kava leaves—fish and roast pig as tender as butter, yams, and queer greens that tasted like nothing Culver ever had eaten before. And there were the draughts of strange drink which

141

Koba continually fetched him in coconut shells.

It had a muddy look and a slimy texture and an odd vegetable taste, but the effect of it was to bring a mindless pleasure to Culver. For a time he was on the verge of song. And then came a period when all the voices sounded loudly and hollowly in his ears, as though he were listening to that roar of the sea which is always imprisoned in a shell. After that, the flames of the fire turned into a queer bright fuzz of obscurity, and finally sleep washed over Culver in delicious waves. A portion of his mind remained clear enough to realize that he was being taken up bodily by two young men and carried, with Koba supporting his head. He knew he was being put down in another place, and that Koba, sitting beside him, gave him a heavenly breeze from the waving of the fan which she held. Then he sank away into a senseless slumber.

CHAPTER 18

Culver wakened with a slightly jarred and vague feeling such as one has when taking another step down and finding the level ground too soon. He was on a shadowy platform outside the hut, sleeping on a mat with a hard roll under his head. He sat up and found Koba curled up beside him with a hand stretched out, almost touching his face. She smiled in her sleep. Some inward impulsion cleared the brain of Culver at once and got him to his feet. The forethought of the girl appeared here, also, for he found beside him a pair of old blue denim trousers and a pair of nondescript shoes which had plenty of room in them for his feet. He was dressed in two gestures and then looked uncertainly around him. The way lay open before him down the hill and he took it. He had a slight sense of guilt when he glanced down at Koba, but he had a greater sense still of liberation.

As he came down through the palms, a group of the islanders saw him and waved and shouted and laughed until he was out of view. He hoped that their voices would not waken Koba from her good sleep. As he neared the lower verge of the grove, he saw the *Spindrift* at anchor with her sails neatly furled and her image beside her in the still water. A small steamer was leaving the bay, trailing its wake back in a distinct line clear to the pier which it had just left. As he came out from the grove, he saw a jumble of boxes and bales on the pier, and native porters clearing them away by degrees. A little tug was tethered to the other side of the pier. Since the pier itself was the apparent center of all life, he went straight toward it.

A little general-merchandise shop near the water front tempted him to step inside with a few questions. A big smoky-eyed halfbreed, in charge, answered no to everything. He had never heard of a Walter Toth. He had heard of Captain Valdez of the *Spindrift,* but if the captain were not on board the ship which then was lying in harbor, he had no idea where the man might be.

Culver went gloomily out to the street—and found himself not three steps from Thomas Wiley and Sally Franklin!

The shock of that sight halted him speechless. They, however, were going straight past him, with an islander behind them, heaped with luggage; the astonishment in his eyes stopped them.

"It's Samuel Culver!" cried Sally. "How could we know you without glasses and brown as a native? Samuel Culver—keep hold of my hand. It's all I have to tell me that I wasn't a fool to jump halfway around the world."

143

"Miss Franklin—or Mrs. Wiley?" said Culver, shaking hands with them.

"Not quite; almost," answered Thomas Wiley. "But what happened to you, Culver? Tell us what it's all about!"

"How did you get on the *Spindrift?* And why?" demanded the girl. "And where is Walter Toth?"

He smiled as he segregated the question into its multiple parts. It was astonishingly pleasant to see them both, but above all to lay eyes on the girl.

"The dog—Napico turned out to be his name," said Culver, "took me at last to the *Spindrift,* at a San Francisco pier; and they wanted the dog on board to follow the trail of his master later on; so they shanghaied me; and I learned on board the ship that your uncle, Walter Toth, had found a large quantity of valuable pearls of which he felt a portion was due to the crew of the *Spindrift* who had assisted him in the past; but the other half he wished to leave to his niece before he died, and death was close to him when he wrote the letter. So I wirelessed to you. It would have been very dangerous to use the sender of the ship again. I had only a few minutes and could not make a long explanation."

"I never heard such a thing as this in my life!" cried the girl. "It's like walking through the mirror and finding the other side of everything."

Culver looked at Wiley, who was beaming broadly, and said: "There are pearls to the value of between six hundred thousand and a million dollars, in the estimation of Walter Toth. And he spoke in the manner of one who knows."

"Six hundred thousand!" said Wiley.

"Half of which would be the right of Miss Franklin," explained Culver. "So that I felt it necessary to send the wireless message."

"Good God, suppose you hadn't!" commented Wiley.

"In the meantime the captain of the *Spindrift,* Valdez, has

144

apparently come ahead of his ship by steam to try to secure all the pearls for himself. But my hope is that for one reason or another he has not yet reached the island.

"Valdez—theft—pearls—the *Spindrift*—a dying man—" said Sally.

"It all would do very well as a fact," answered Culver, "except for the mention of the pearls, don't you agree? They remove the whole matter into the realm of fiction. I've often thought of that. The dog, the ship, Valdez, the dying man— we could believe all of that, but when we come to buried treasure, so to speak, the thing is at once incredible. Perhaps modern financiers have taught us to believe that money cannot be found except through compound interest? And who is the poet who says:

> In daylight all the midnight marvels die;
> Wonders are for the ear, not for the eye.

"Poets to quote—even on Tapua—even in the middle of a melodrama," murmured the girl. "Didn't I tell you so, Tommy? But where did you pick up that red scar on your forehead, please?"

"As a matter of fact, that was how I was introduced to life on the *Spindrift*," explained Culver. "Sailors are a bit abrupt in their manners; particularly the crew of the *Spindrift*. Shall we go on to your lodgings?"

They went on, slowly, walking continually sidewise to continue questions and answers. Thomas Wiley by the grace of chance had been at his wireless when the message arrived; but it was hardly grace of chance that he had had it tuned so fine that he caught the vague whisper of the key across those thousand of miles of ocean. It had been almost a perfect day for reception, he said, otherwise the thing could not have come through. He had gone at once with the wild news to Sally Franklin. They waited a day or two for a confirming

145

message. Then they heard that the big liner *Norman Prince* was sailing at once for the South Seas and touched at Wago, near Tapua, with steamship connections between the two islands. That news had decided them to go. They almost had taken out a marriage license first.

"But she still hasn't quite made up her mind about me," said Thomas Wiley. "She doesn't know me well enough. Only ten years or so. Ten years more and I might be able to pull the thing off."

"But that, actually—that beautiful ship in the harbor—is that the *Spindrift* which you came on?"

"The very same. We arrived last night," explained Culver.

"And are those shore clothes for a sailor?"

"These are only accidents," he told her calmly. "I had to leave the ship in a hurry and swim ashore. And since it means we have met in this fashion—"

He broke off short because around the next corner of the "English" district of Tapua came the magnificence of Napico with his nose close to the ground, then again with head high in the air. Holding him were Alec and Jemmison, with Burke in person to the rear, still conning his craft from the poop deck, as it were. They had not succeeded in putting the muzzle on the big dog. Instead, they handled him with a pair of strong lines which were rove into his collar. Walking well out from him and taking no chances with his teeth, the two strong men kept him at a distance while they escorted him through the town, plainly with the hope that he might pick up the trail of Valdez.

"Napico!" cried out big Culver.

It was a mere exclamation, not a call; for the dog never had answered to his name before, when Culver spoke it. This time there was a difference. Napico halted, looked quickly around him, spotted Culver, and went for him with a lunge.

146

Perhaps Culver looked to the beast like a port in a storm. His heavy lunge was checked at once by the twin lines which controlled him. He flew into a snarling passion at once. First he lurched toward the legs of Alec with a side-slash of his fangs, and missing that target, he took up the slack in the opposite direction by flinging himself at Jemmison.

Perhaps Alec would have held him safely enough. But Jemmison dropped his line with a shout; Napico whipped the other rope through the hands of Alec, and in a moment the big dog was at the feet of Culver. There he turned around and faced his enemies with a bristling hatred. Burke was enriching the air with an amazing flow of language, consigning Alec and Jemmison to various hells. Culver picked up the fallen ropes and held Napico on a short leash.

"Walk right on," he said to Wiley and the startled face of Sally. "It's all right. . . . Only give him plenty of headroom; don't let him come within reaching distance of you. But he's as much my dog as he is theirs. . . . Good morning, Alec!"

He went on slowly, still holding the dog short. He could not see either of the other faces but only that of Burke, who gave aside when Culver came closer. Probably it was not fear of Culver's hands but the teeth of the dog that backed him up. At any rate, he gave them a clear passage. His voice did not return to him until they were several steps past him and then he shouted: "I'll have it out of you, Culver! I'll have you back on board and I'll break you, Culver!"

That was all. The porter shambled ahead and showed them the way around the next corner.

"Who is that?" breathed Sally. "Who in the world is that?"

"That's Burke," said Culver. He looked at the girl strangely; there was a world, an entire world that he had passed around since he last saw her, and Burke had been the highest pinnacle in it. He had learned an entirely new lesson from Burke and that was how to hate. He despised himself for feeling that unworthy passion, but he could not help a sense that hatred was something like carbon in iron—it enabled the human metal to take a sharper edge and hold it longer. Hate, for instance, was what had led Burke so patiently on the long back trail of Valdez. "Burke," added Culver, "who commands the *Spindrift* while the captain is away from her. Burke, who is following Valdez. And whether he or Valdez reaches Toth first, you never will see your share of the pearls."

"But he is the man who stopped and asked me about Uncle Walter that day in San Francisco!" said the girl. "It's beginning to give me chills, Tommy. The wheel is turning around full circle, and I'm seeing some of the first spokes of it again!"

They got to a "hotel," which was a one-story shack patronized by sailors. There was no other public lodging place in Tapua, and while Tommy Wiley went in to look at rooms, Culver remained outside with Napico. The big dog was too dangerous to take into an unknown place among unknown people without a muzzle. Sally remained outside with Culver.

There had been no wind to speak of but now the fronds of the palms began to shake and the soft, humid air stirred. The nose of Napico thrust out into it at once; he began to strain toward the inner side of the walk. When Culver let him move there, his nose instantly was on the ground. He began to whine, and to the astonishment of Culver, his shaggy tail started wagging.

"He's found something important to him," said Culver. "I'll see where this goes—"

Napico was trying to gallop on the trail. He swung his head about and snarled at the restraining ropes.

"Be careful!" the girl warned him. "How can you stay

close to that green-eyed devil? He's a regular Chinese dragon, I think. Watch him, please!"

Napico towed Culver down the street at a good pace, turned a corner, and mounted the steps of a little bungalow which was set back behind an excuse for a garden. It was a dilapidated cottage with a great need of white paint to freshen its face. Napico raged until he got to the front door and stood up scratching at it with his forepaws until Culver pulled him back. His eagerness hurt Culver with a singular pain, but he found the hard grip of excitement on him at the same time. Valdez, he thought—only for Valdez would the dog show this tense desire to go on. And Valdez was the man whom Culver wished to face; but in that meeting Napico would pass out of his hands forever.

The girl felt the tension, also.

"Does it mean something now, this moment?" she asked. "Shall I run back for Tommy?"

"Let Tommy be," answered Culver shortly, for he was feeling that he was a mere weed in the grass, something to be plucked up and thrown away. If he found Valdez, the dog left him; and now he served Sally in order that young Tommy should take her. He was rather amazed to find this thought in his mind, and hastily he told himself, as he knocked at the door, that she was young, very young, and he was old. He was thirty-five; he was in middle age; and more than years had aged him still more. What share had he in rewards? His reward, indeed, would probably be the scattering of the library which he had collected with such pain during years, perhaps even his cupboard stacked with the scholarly notations of his life would be thrown into the junk heap by Mrs. Lindley when she made the room ready for another guest! He was roused from this unhappy trance by the sudden tugging of Napico to get into the house.

149

The door was open, and a man in an undershirt, with wrinkled, bagging white trousers, and bare feet, stood in the hallway holding the door.

"What's the main idea?" he asked. "I don't keep dogs here. Back that brute outside. You need a stable for him, anyway. He's big enough to pass for a horse."

"He seems," said Culver politely, "to be following a trail. He seems to know someone who is in the place."

"That's me," said the stranger. "I'm the only man in the house."

"There might be a woman, perhaps?" asked Culver, with a dying hope.

"I'll be damned if there is or ever will be. I've had my fill of them, let me tell you."

He had the tattooed forearms of a sailor. A scrub of two days' beard gave a moldy look to his face, for the hair was spotted with gray. He was as round and heavy as a section sawed out of a big log.

"Do you know a Captain Valdez?" asked the girl suddenly.

The man in the hall moved until he could look past Culver.

"Sorry, ma'am," he said. "I didn't see you out there. What Valdez would you be meaning?"

"The one who used to be the captain of the *Spindrift*," she said.

"Oh, him?" repeated the sailor. "Sure I've heard of him, but I never laid eyes on his face. He keeps a hard ship, I'm told. There's the *Spindrift* out in the harbor now, they tell me. What about Valdez?"

"I thought," said Culver, "that this dog would never follow a trail as he's following this one, unless it were the trail of Valdez. He belongs to the Captain."

"Well, there's no captain here," answered the sailor.

"None here, and ain't been."

Culver looked calmly at him.

"Has someone come into your house from the street this morning?" he asked.

"Not a soul."

"Yesterday?"

"How the hell can I remember everything and everybody that might of come in here?" demanded the sailor. "And who are you? And what d'you want?"

"I don't look like the police, do I?" asked Culver, smiling.

The sailor almost jerked the door shut. He demanded through the narrowing crack of it: "What have I got to think about police for?"

"That," said Culver, "is your own concern, and not mine. I can't say what the police will think or do, of course. Who is it that says:

> Fear lays its ugly shadow on the floor,
> Taps at the window, breathes beneath the
> door.

"Who talks about fear?" asked the sailor, jerking the door open again. "There wasn't anything phoney about this dying. God knows he was long enough at it and the whole town could of known, if it wanted to come here and take a look. If it wanted to ask questions, it could of asked them. I buried him right out in the open in the graveyard, didn't I?"

"My dear friend, I'm accusing you of nothing," said Culver.

"Are you a lawyer or something?" asked the sailor. "What've you come here for?"

"To ask for permission for my dog to get into your house," said Culver. "Do you definitely refuse me entrance?"

This question was a puzzler to the sailor. His brow gathered into a black scowl. He looked for a moment as though he might be about to use his foot on Napico or his fist on Culver; then he stepped back and said: "O.K. Come on in. But don't hang around about it. Get him in and get him out again, and it's all damned foolishness to me, I'm telling you."

Napico went straight in, scratching the floor loudly with his claws as he pulled heavily against the lead. He turned at once to the right, bumped open an almost closed door with his shoulder, and exposed a neat little bedroom to view. It was done up with the tidiness of a sailor, a blanket folded across the end of the narrow cot, the matting clean, the woodwork obviously washed very recently.

"This is the place, is it?" asked Culver. "This is the place, I see."

"What of it?" asked the sailor. "Ain't it good enough?"

"That depends, perhaps," said Culver, "on the purpose to which it is put."

"Why the hell don't you come right out and say what you're thinking about me?" asked the host. "Say: 'Parker, I think you're a thief'; or, 'Parker, I think you're a crook'; or, 'Parker, I think it's murder!' Why don't you come out and say what you think, man?"

The man was breathing hard and he stood with his legs braced well apart and a fighting look on his face.

"I'd be foolish to accuse a man until there's a crime known," Culver said.

"You're one of these Government birds," stated Parker. "You're one of those damned slickers that come snooping around and making trouble wherever you go. You think you're disguised, don't you? Hell, yes, you're wearing old jeans and shoes that don't match and you think that makes a beachcomber out of you. But I'll tell you that the first

152

word out of your mouth, I spotted you for somebody higher up. College. I knew it was somebody yapping college talk. With my eyes closed I could've told by your lingo."

"I'm sorry," said Culver. "I shouldn't be so apparent, it seems."

"Yeah, I ain't so dumb," admitted Parker. "But go on and look. There's the bed that he died in. Here's the room that he lived in. Now go ahead and try to make something of it, will you?" And he broke out: "Murder! That's what you think! I can see it in your look. Murder! Go on and tell me that's what you think!"

Sally Franklin shrank back a bit toward the door. The dog, in the meantime, had been sniffing here and there about the floor, his tail slowly wagging, his ruff bristling with his excitement.

Now he took a sudden turn and pushed his head inside the door of an open, shallow closet. He reappeared again, carrying in his mouth a much-scuffed slipper which was downtrodden at the heel.

"How the devil—" began Parker, and then shut himself up by striking his right hand quickly against his mouth.

Culver said nothing. He watched Parker silently, while Napico sat down on the floor with the slipper between his paws and guarded it, whining with a happy contentment.

"Matter of fact—" began Parker, and then he paused again with color beginning to rise in his face.

"And did that belong to the dead man?" asked Culver.

"Damn the dog!" cried out Parker. He looked toward the window and then toward the door. At last he said: "Well, suppose it was the other one?"

"What other one?" asked Culver.

"You don't know, eh?" commented Parker, sneering. "No, not much you don't! You couldn't guess, could you?"

"I hoped that you'd help me out," answered Culver.

153

"All right. He acted like he wanted to keep it dark, but why should I wind up in the hoosegow on account of him? All right. There was somebody else here most of the time; there was Van Zandt!"

Having said this, he heaved up both arms and let them fall heavily to his side, as a sign that he had resisted as long as he could but had to surrender at last.

"Parker," said Culver, "let me take a weight off your mind. I'm not here to bring up your past before your eyes. I merely hope that you'll give me a reasonable assistance."

"Well?" growled Parker.

"After all, he did not give you enough money to make you rich?" suggested Culver.

Parker blinked. Then he exclaimed: "I wish I'd shoved the money down his throat! Now, what do you want out of me?"

"Your dead man is buried—but tell me how long his friend was at your house?" asked Culver.

"Three, four weeks, maybe. There was a week before that when he just come to visit every day. I dunno what kind of a friend he was. My sick man told me to keep him out, after the first couple of times."

"But Van Zandt had money enough to buy his way in, of course?"

"Look here," answered Parker, black with his scowl again and sweating under the inquisition, "I gotta make a living, don't I? I ain't here for my health."

"Suppose you describe Van Zandt for me?" Culver suggested.

"I guess you know what he looks like," replied Parker. "A beak and a chin like he wears ain't seen every day; and you don't get two hundred and fifty pounds of man wrapped up in one suit of clothes every day of your life, do you?"

"No," answered Culver. "That is rare, of course. . . .

154

May we be alone in here for a short time?"

"As long as you want," said Parker, and went out of the room, leaving Culver at a stand, dreaming. For he was remembering the Roman, imperial profile and the huge bulk of the man in the automobile Napico had vainly pursued that night in San Francisco, which seemed two or three lifetimes in the buried past. Not Van Zandt, but Valdez must be the name, and he had come close to the end of the trail at last.

CHAPTER 19

He said to the girl: "Shouldn't you go back to Tommy and tell him where we are?"

"Go back? Leave this?" she asked. "I've never lived a step or a word or a thought before in my whole life! Leave this? I can't leave it! Tell me what you think. Van Zandt—who is Van Zandt?"

"Valdez, probably," replied Culver.

"And the dead man?"

"That has to be your uncle, I suppose."

Something took the place of the excitement in her eyes.

"He was a queer, jolly, happy man," she said. "And everyone always was afraid that he would come home drunk. But he's dead; and he was my uncle!"

"Interesting," said Culver. "Presently you will reason yourself into a state of grief because of a stranger."

"Please don't!" she said, angered a little.

"I beg your pardon," said Culver. "I merely was noticing the response which society labors to exact from us; we are forced into a conventional reaction. That was what interested me so much in your remark. I could see that you were proceeding through logic toward tears."

She laughed, briefly, and then watched him with curious, almost frightened eyes. "There's something rather terrible about you, you know," she said. "I'd hate to be cornered by you as poor Parker was."

"Terrible?" he repeated, amazed.

"I meet a very gentle man," she said, "who lives inside of great walls of books and peers out at the world through thick glasses. The same man goes down to the sea; I don't know how many storms and men beat on him, but he comes up from the sea again with his eyes young once more, and wearing a scar and a queer little smile of contentment as though everything had been simply another chapter out of a book." Her voice changed as she asked: "How were you so sure that Valdez had been here?"

"I was not sure at all. I was fumbling in the blindest darkness," explained Culver. "But Napico was very sure indeed."

"Might it not have been another trail than that of Valdez?"

"What trail but that of Valdez would make Napico whine and wag his tail?"

The dog, in fact, looked up with another whine from the slipper, when he heard the name of his master.

"But you knew that the sailor had a past that would make him afraid of the law; and you asked questions as though you were an officer of the law. Are you, Samuel Culver? Are you in the secret police?"

"No," he answered. "As for Parker's past, I saw that questions worried him. The poet says:

> Sin, once invited, dwells within our eyes
> And views the future with a dark surmise.

156

"It was Parker's uneasy conscience that troubled him more than my questions."

"Ah, but you make everything easy with your quotations from the poets, as though they did all your thinking for you."

"There are a hundred generations of the poets," he said, "and what they say of the past must be true of the present, until human nature changes."

"What do you think has happened?"

"Valdez came and found Toth very ill. He pretended that he represented the entire crew of sailors who had helped Toth, but Toth doubted that. He even wished to keep Valdez out of his room, after two visits. But Valdez bribed Parker and kept coming. He wanted to learn the secret; he kept pressing to find out where the pearls of Mullaley had been hidden in the forest; and still week after week Toth doubted him and resisted. Until, I suppose, Toth felt that death was upon him, the other day. And then he talked rather than let the pearls disappear from the face of the world!"

"So Valdez has gone for them, now?" she asked. "What can we do?"

"Follow him, I suppose," said Culver.

"But where? Which way has he gone? There are a thousand trails leading back into the interior of Tapua, aren't there?"

"We'll have to find some indication here," answered Culver.

"There isn't an indication," she said. "There's nothing in the room except that slipper, and this silly magazine and the novel, there, and the calendar pad."

"There are only those three things," agreed Culver. "So we'll have to study them page by page. Will you take the calendar while I take the magazine?"

157

She was about to protest but there was a calm certainty about Culver that gave his words a certain force. She saw him pick up the magazine and start turning the pages. So, in her turn, she took the calendar and went rapidly through it.

"There's nothing in it. Every page is a blank," she said, looking up.

She discovered that Culver was only beginning the magazine and had hardly turned half a dozen sheets of it.

He said: "Will you tell Thomas Wiley where we are? He'll be worried."

"But Valdez!" she exclaimed. "Every moment he is getting farther and farther away from us. We'll never find him!"

"Every moment it grows more difficult," he admitted; "but we must study the page to find out the meaning. It is a time for quiet and thought, I dare say. But we have to have food for thought, you know, and that's what I'm trying to find. Will you tell Wiley?"

She hurried from the place and fairly ran to the little lodging house where Thomas Wiley was pacing impatiently up and down in front of the place.

She told him the news briefly.

"But he's found a book and now he's lost himself in print!" she said. "He'll be no use to us now. Tommy, start out through the town and ask questions everywhere. Ask if Valdez has been seen, and where he was going. A huge man of two hundred and fifty pounds with a great chin and a beak of a nose. I'll go back to Samuel Culver, but I'm afraid that he'll be no help now. . . . He's nibbling at printed words like a mouse at a granary, and he'll never be through!"

In fact, when she returned to the house and Parker had walked into the front room, Culver was sitting with the calendar open in front of him, absently shading a page with light strokes of a pencil stub which he had picked up. Perhaps this was to assist the operations of his mind, by occupying his hands, she thought! She controlled her impatience, saying mildly: "Have you had any luck? Have you found anything?"

"About your uncle? A great deal," said Culver. "And if he were still above ground the facts might be useful!"

"Facts about him? I remembered him a little. Will you tell me what you've found out?" she wanted to know, still keeping her voice steady by force of great effort.

"He was an elderly fellow and women played no great part in his life," said Culver. "Adventure was what he loved. He was a chatty man, and loved to talk. Besides, he was careless and very nervous; an incessant smoker; and, toward the end at least, he was extremely unhappy. Despairing, I might say."

"Have you found a letter he wrote? How on earth do you know all this?"

"By studying the pages," said Culver. "Ashes between nearly all of them, the love stories hardly thumbed, the adventure yarns well finger-rubbed, and particularly the pages of dialogue. He had had this magazine as a companion for a long time. Sometimes he threw it aside, crumpling the corners. Sometimes he dropped it face down, even in the exciting middle of an adventure."

"It's all true, as I remember him," she said, staring. "But have you given up hope now? Are you sitting there trying to find a ghost of a clue for us to follow by thinking about it?"

"Well, it's a little more than a ghost of a clue," answered Culver. "You see?"

He tore out the page from the calendar and held it out to her. "He was dying, or almost dying, when he made it," pointed out Culver. "You see how the lines waver, and how

159

they are clear in one place and dim in another and fade out altogether later on?"

The light pencil strokes had covered the paper with a film of gray lead which brought out into relief a number of slight indentations, which formed lines and two or three arrows. All of one side was a blank except for a few faint indications. This was the tracery left by a drawing made on the page above.

"Those two upward strokes at the top," said Culver, "probably mean the volcano, Tapua itself. And the arrow points to the left, that is, to the northern side of the volcano. And this wavering line perhaps indicates a trail, spotted by the arrow."

"It's true!" exclaimed the girl. "But all this part is a blank!"

"His hand was growing weak and scrawling, by that time."

"Then we have only the vague beginning of the trail, and nothing to follow on toward the end?" asked Sally.

"If we can come to that vague beginning, perhaps Napico would help us the rest of the way," suggested Culver.

"Then let's hurry. Let's go now!"

"I was about to say the same thing," replied Culver, and stood up with the dog.

The moment he started for the door, Napico, as though he understood what sort of game was afoot, dropped the slipper and became bright-eyed wth excitement.

"And Tommy?" asked Culver, as they walked up through the village, and into the tangled scrub beyond it, pointing just left of the north shoulder of Mount Tapua. "Should Tommy be with us?"

"If we find a trail, I'll run back for him—don't stop now!" pleaded Sally. "You will find it. I know you will. I'm almost sorry for Valdez, now. I suppose he was sure to be caught from the moment you turned your mind in his direction. Tell me, honestly—it isn't the first time you've done something like this, is it?"

"I've done nothing," answered Culver, "except work with books; but for a student there are a thousand hard trails to follow and dimmer indications than are on this map, a great deal. Suppose you are trying to follow a thought or a characteristic of a writer who is revealing himself only unconsciously in his words. How can a human being hide himself on the face of the earth as easily as thought can be hidden in the huge universe of the mind?"

The dog, as he spoke, pulled violently to the left as another trail joined the one they were walking on. The nose of Napico went down at once. His head wavered from side to side, following an exact scent; and he strained at the lead with trembling haunches. That faint whine, which Culver had heard before, began to come from the throat of the big fellow.

"He has it!" said the girl. "He has it! He has it!"

She caught Culver's arm and fairly danced with excitement, looking up and laughing into his face in a full abandonment of happiness. Then the pale green growth beside the trail parted and Culver looked askance into the face of Koba.

Koba made a fine statue against the background of green. For she was wearing a grass skirt and several chains of bright beads. Not even shoes encumbered her. She had her arms folded high, with an imperial demeanor. When she was most furiously bad-tempered, she was sure to smile a little, and she was smiling now in a way that chilled the blood of Culver. He was already walking past her with Sally when she appeared. Sally, rather startled, gasped a moment later: "What a beauty! But great heavens, does she know you?"

Koba, in her husky voice, was speaking rapidly, her eyes turning after Culver, but in her excitement she was using

161

only her native tongue. Nevertheless her meaning was not altogether lost. Her language had the same fine terminal trill that is unmistakable in the cursing of an Irishman.

Culver said: "Koba, what's the matter?"

"Thief!" cried Koba, remembering her English. "Thief! Thief! Thief!"

And she pressed both hands over her heart, to make clear just what he had stolen. Culver retreated inch by inch before her passion, and Koba went into a queer, primitive dance. It consisted of kicking the ground rapidly with her heels and shaking her fists at the earth, the sky, and Culver.

"White pig! White pig! White pig!" screamed Koba. "May her children have hair on their faces—hair on their faces—hair on their faces!"

Culver rounded a sudden corner of the trail, pulled on by the lunging of Napico. Now that he was out of sight of Koba, he legged it swiftly to increase the distance.

"What a lovely girl—and what a warm manner she has!" said Sally. "Have you known her long?"

"Not very," said Culver.

"Not long, but well, I suppose," said Sally. "What a golden goddess! And yet not so little, either. Would you say."

"A hundred and thirty pounds, I dare say," said Culver, brooding.

To see Koba in such a transport of rage was something like seeing lightning at noonday. It was hard to remember, suddenly, how she had been the other night when they were walking up through the palm grove and in the whole world there had seemed only one lovely thing.

"A hundred and thirty pounds? You do know her well," commented Sally, with an odd lilt in her voice. "What was she saying at first in her own tongue?"

"I don't know," sighed Culver.

"I think you missed something," said Sally. "It had a very authentic sort of a sound. How lovely she is, the golden against the green. I didn't know you had such an eye for beauty."

"I can't tell why it is," said Culver, "but what you say makes me unhappy."

He looked suddenly askance at her and saw that she was smiling, and yet there was something more than mirth in her face.

"Shall I tell you about Koba?" he asked.

"Please," said the girl.

She glanced over her shoulder. He had the same unhappy feeling that perhaps Koba might be following them, and knowing her as he did, he would rather have been followed by a snake.

"There was a time of trouble on the ship," said Culver, "and she helped me."

"I think she could be a very efficient helper," said Sally.

"My back was raw," he told her, "and Koba rubbed it with an unguent of some sort."

"How sweet of her," said Sally. "Was it a bad sunburn or something?"

The memory came over him and turned him to stone. He stood still, and even the frantic lunges of Napico did not stir him any more than though they had been wireless tremors in the air.

"It was not sunburn," said Culver, in a new, hard voice. "But I was—" He stopped to get breath. He needed air.

"Never mind. Please don't!" said Sally, looking up at him alarmedly.

But he started and the thing that was lodged in his throat had to come out. Perhaps if he spoke it, the throttling hate would leave him once for all.

163

"I had my wrists tied up in the rigging," he said slowly. "And then, I was flogged, with a whip, as a mule or a dog is flogged—with a whip. Helpless!"

The girl said nothing. She had moved back from him a little. He remained standing still.

"Afterward," he said, in the same hard, slow voice, "I walked the deck of that ship and obeyed orders. I saw the man who flogged me, and I did nothing about it. I saw him walking the poop and conning the ship, and I let him pass. Yet he had flogged me. Like a dog!"

He rubbed a hand across his forehead.

Then he said, controlling himself so that his voice was normal again: "Afterward, she came forward into the forecastle and rubbed my back with the ointment. She sang to me, and told me what the songs meant, and I went to sleep."

"I should think you'd love her!" cried Sally.

He thought for a moment.

"Almost," he said. "Almost."

"But really—with all your heart!"

"I think there was someone in my heart before her," said Culver in his simple way.

Sally said no more. Instead of asking him to explain, she walked on, her eyes thoughtfully on the toes of her shoes.

CHAPTER 20

Culver became conscious of the darkening of the sun, and he saw that the trail had entered a great tunnel of green. Huge fronds of palms joined overhead; climbing vines like agile, swiftly twisting snakes, ran up the stems and disappeared; graceful flowing plants hung down from above.

In that pleasant shade he stopped and looked at Sally. She was red-faced and sweating with the hard work of keeping up with his long strides.

"There's Wiley to think of!" he told her. "You've got to go back to him at once. Suppose we meet Valdez? That wouldn't be the place for you!"

"Suppose you meet Valdez," said the girl, "what will you do—with your empty hands?"

"I would talk," said Culver calmly.

"And suppose that there should have to be more than talk? Suppose that Napico took the side of his master? And suppose that you— What would you do?"

"Pico?" said Culver absently.

The dog turned his head and flashed an impatient glance behind him. Then he wagged his tail and lurched against the rope.

But Culver held him firmly.

"It has to come," he said. "Pico has to make a choice between us; and of course he'll choose his master. Of course he will. What else can he do?"

"Does he mean that much to you?" asked the girl.

"I don't know," said Culver. "I don't know how much he means to me. I won't know until he's gone. Then I'll be able to tell you, quite eloquently, I imagine. He's only a dog; but he managed to break through to me. You see, I was living inside walls. They were not even glass walls. I could not see what the rest of the world was doing. Napico, here—well, he dragged me out of thousands of years of the past, and I found myself all at once in the present. Instead of looking at words, I was looking at life. I have a new taste in my throat."

He laughed a little.

"I don't know how to put it," he said. "But suppose, one

165

day, Napico came of his own free will and put his head in my hand?"

"I can see that that would be a great day," murmured the girl.

"Yes," agreed Culver. "It would be a great day. . . . But now you've got to go back to Tom Wiley."

"Do you realize how many times the trails have crossed in the last half-hour?" she asked. "You were striding along alone with your thoughts; but do you realize that I never could get back alone?"

"I didn't realize that," he admitted. "Is there nothing to do but take you along?"

"Nothing, I'm afraid," she said. She took out a handkerchief and mopped her face. "Do we have to go quite so fast?" she begged.

"Certainly not," said Culver. "They are not very far ahead of us."

"They?" she queried.

"There are two. There is the big man—you see where his heel crunched down through the upper crust of the ground: And then there is this."

He pointed out the print of a naked foot, lightly made.

"A woman?" she asked.

"It's too big for a woman," said Culver. "You see how the big toe gripped the ground? That's a man's foot—the foot of a man who's a runner. The big toe gives a great deal of the spring to a runner's stride, you know."

"Is there any poetry to quote for that?" she asked.

"There is Shakespeare," he said, innocent of her faint smile, "when he speaks of Diomedes' step, rising aspiring on his toes. And someone wrote:

> He rounds the hill; he runs upon the air
> And the far towers prick up beneath his
> feet.

166

"Is there poetry for everything, then?" she asked.

"Perhaps there is," he said. "And in the past—that is, before Napico—I used to think that everything had been said that needed saying."

"But now?" she queried.

"Well, now there have been times when the old poets failed me, and I wished that I could write my own lines," said Culver.

"Tell me about that, won't you?" asked the girl.

She had taken off her hat to let the faint stirring of the air cool her more.

"Well," said Culver, "I've wanted lines even about the color of your hair. And particularly from that night you were in my room, I remember a sort of freshness and a happiness around the heart."

She looked past him with considering eyes. "I too remember that night wonderfully well, and I'll never forget some of the things you said," she told him.

"You cautioned me not to speak like that to any other person," said Culver, recalling the conversation suddenly. "But as a matter of fact, I never have." He smiled as he examined his recollection and found it clear. "Because the truth is," he said, "that I've never felt that way before, and never will again. It was a strange beauty that came to me from you—like the beauty of classic verse: the wings of Pindar, you know, and the melancholy that always goes with a pure loveliness, and which you feel in music at once."

"And Koba—did she never make you happy?" persisted Sally Franklin.

"Let me see. . . . There was once on the ship. She wore an odd fragrance, a perfume which her mother's grandmother, as I remember it, had made and left the secret of making in the family. It had a strange effect of making the head a little dizzy."

"I'll wager it did. Didn't you talk to Koba then?"

"No," he answered, thinking back to the moment.

"You try to remember," said Sally, with a peculiar confidence, "and you'll find that once at least you told Koba how happy she was making you."

"There was last night," he agreed, as the moment came back to him.

"Ah, I knew," said Sally.

"There was a sound of wind like surf in the trees, and her husky voice blended with it and seemed to express the same thought," said Culver.

"What thought?" asked Sally.

"The thought of peace at the end of the day, and quiet and happy homecoming. As we walked, I recalled her on the ship, and swimming in the lagoon. She has, as you may have observed, an extraordinarily lovely body."

"Yes, extraordinary," said the girl, watching him.

"And as we walked under the palms with the moonlight making the world silver white and soft black, I remembered her in many pictures."

"So you told her about them?"

"At some length," said Culver.

"And what did she do?"

"Practically nothing. While I was talking, she merely sang."

"She sang while you talked?"

"Yes. She sang, softly. Almost like an accompaniment. It showed that her mind was not on what I was saying, of course."

"Poor Koba!" said Sally.

"Poor Koba?" he echoed, surprised.

"I think I know about her now," sighed Sally Franklin.

"You must not judge her entirely from her anger when we passed her," said Culver. "That was inexplicable; but the unschooled brain is capable of vagaries, as you know."

168

"I do know," she answered. "And some schooled minds also. Poor Koba!"

"I wonder," said Culver, "if you're implying that I did something wrong about her?"

"Yes. Wrong as the very devil," said Sally.

"You don't mean it!" exclaimed Culver. He grew extremely hot of face. "I'm not unaware," he said, "that native women are capable of unusual latitude in some of their actions. Their moral sense has not been cultivated. Koba, however, is not of that type. I gathered that even the great Valdez—and his is a great name at sea—did not have his way with her. I beg your pardon. I'm sorry to mention this."

"I was born in the twentieth century, my dear," said Sally calmly.

He felt that he was driven to an explicit statement. It was difficult to bring out the words, but he forced himself to them.

"The truth is," he said, "that I did not touch her!"

"Oh, no! You didn't touch her body. But what about her mind and soul? What about them?"

"Will you please explain?" begged Culver in an agony of apprehension, he hardly knew of what.

"I can't explain," she said.

"Surely there would be some words—" he tried to say.

"No, there aren't any," she snapped. "How old are you, please?"

"I am thirty-five," he confessed.

"Are you? Without glasses, you don't look it. You look hardly more than a boy. And sometimes I think that you are less than a boy; because in spite of all your books, you are so desperately—ignorant!"

She selected the word deliberately, and he winced.

"Perhaps I am—I dare say I am," admitted Culver.

169

"Don't be humble!" she exclaimed.

"I'm only telling you, with honesty, what's in my mind. If you could explain what I've done wrong—"

"But I tell you, I can't explain!"

He took a deep breath and closed his eyes. The pain that was in him was unlike anything he ever had known. The whip in the hands of Burke had scarified the flesh only. Here, if he could draw her into words, might be found the explanation of all the differences he had felt, his whole life, between him and other men. But she would not speak! Even the quest of Valdez seemed as nothing compared to this Wishing Gate which he had reached, and found the lips of the oracle dumb!

"You are very angry," said Culver slowly, feeling his way forward through the dark jungle of his thoughts. "And in the world there is only one person whose anger I would wish to avoid, it seems to me. I don't know how to explain. But the days at sea, and the shame and the anxiety, have been seeming like a bad dream. . . . Did you ever spend a sleepless night and think of follies and shames until morning came?"

"I have," she answered, frowning.

"And when the dawn came, there is a coolness in the air, and a quiet. If the wind has blown all night long, it dies out in the morning, as a rule, and coldness and the peace seems to come from heaven. It puts a hand on your forehead and on your heart, don't you think?"

"I know," she nodded, still frowning.

"You were that for me when I saw you in Tapua," said Culver.

"Ah, there you go again!" she cried.

"I'm only telling you the utter truth. Can't I speak it?"

"I suppose I have to hear it now," she murmured, looking away from him.

"But it's true," said Culver, "that when I saw you, there

170

was a pause in time. The whole universe stood still for me, and I heard music in the silence. It's strange, isn't it? It was like music; looking at you was like that for me."

"Tell me," said the girl; "do you know that I'm engaged to Tommy Wiley?"

"I do know it," he said, and waited.

"Do you think he loves me, truly?"

"I think he does," said Culver honestly, looking back to certain expressions which he had seen in the face of that young man, and remembering certain qualities of voice.

"Then would his heart be rather broken if I turned him away?"

"I dare say," agreed Culver, still waiting anxiously for the key to this talk.

"Could you go on talking to me as you were just talking now—a moment ago?"

"As long as I'm near you," said Culver. He hunted in his mind for an image; and finding it, he said: "Are you ever weary of watching seagulls in the wind, going up hills and down valleys in the air, and turning sharp corners in the streets of some invisible happy city? Are you ever weary of watching them? Well, the truth is that it's like that, and I'm never weary of watching you and listening, no matter what you say, or what you do with your hands."

"If I'm not to wring Tommy's heart, and turn him away, don't say another word!"

Culver, amazed, was beyond words.

"It shall be exactly as you wish," he said at last.

"Could you find something out of your poets to tell me what is in your mind just now?"

"I can only think of this," he said:

> The thought of her comes to me like the fall
> Of dew that gilds the morning, like the fall
> Of rain in the hot, dusty throat of August;

171

Like wings between the morning and the
    night
She comes to me; but only in my thought.

She considered this for a long moment, and then, sighing,
turned to take up the trail. He went ahead with the dog. He
could not understand women!

CHAPTER 21

Now that she had confessed her weariness, he went on
more slowly in consideration of her. It seemed strange to
Culver that she should lack physical strength, because in
his mind's eye he considered her complete, perfect, armed
at every point like a true Achilles, the swiftest, the most
tireless, the most terrible of the Greeks. And in that old
Greek conception which placed such qualities apparently
above all moral considerations of character, it seemed to
him that he found a right place for the girl. Such people
are inexplicable. Culver would give up attempting to understand. She chose to marry the clear-eyed lad Tommy Wiley.
Therefore it should be so. Her will was sufficient unto herself, and it would have to be sufficient unto him. He accepted blindly, but with a certain remorseless aching of the
heart. He tried, as he went down the dimness of the trail
behind Napico, to think back to his days of books; but they
seemed far away, hidden in a dust cloud and a rattling of
dead leaves.

He was half adrift in these struggles of the mind, when
the dog for the first time lifted his nose from the ground,
and as though he had the quarry in view, strained forward

with a high head. They were in a scene like a romantic stage set, the backdrop consisting of a cliff set back in terraces, with a decoration of tropical green on each terrace. A stream of water pitched over the top of the highest terrace, and leaped down step by step until in the lowest step of all, the trade wind took the shattered column and blew it aside into a mist that fell soundlessly. There was a noise of thunder, therefore; but it hung always above them in the sky; the nearer sound was a continual hushing of soft rain.

The dog went straight on toward the cliff. Near two large trees which leaned together as if for mutual support, Napico struck a stand like a pointing dog, his head thrusting forward, his eyes almost closed as he studied the wind and growled, his big ruff bristling.

The girl saw first, and cried out. After that, Culver made out a glimpse of a brown body stretched in the deep grass between the two trees, with the head turned, and the half-shut eyes peering out at him. There was a purple blotch in the center of the forehead.

Napico, pulling to the end of his lead, sniffed once at the dead man, then turned at right angles and tried to make away through the grass.

Valdez had come with a guide, but had gone by himself! At the foot of one of the trees lay a small heap of rotten wood fiber and earth that had been scraped out of a hollow in the trunk. That must have been the hiding place selected by Walter Toth. No doubt the islander who guided Toth had had a glimpse of what was taken from the cache, and Valdez had decided that it would be impossible to let him keep the information and live.

Culver looked up along the new trail of Valdez toward the green wall of the jungle. The foliage, wavering in the wind, had a new significance, because it might be covering the watchful eyes of Valdez at that moment. He looked back to the dead man. The half-open eyes still seemed to consider the world with puzzled concern.

"Are you all right, Sally?" Culver asked, not daring to look at her.

"I'm all right," she answered in a muffled voice. "But look there, look there! They've found us! What will they do?"

Koba came first, walking lightly, like one about to break into a run. An air of triumph made her seem taller, and in fact she had won an important race. The weakness of Sally Franklin, which had slowed Culver so much on the trail, the foolishness of high heels and binding skirts, might be the ruin of them both now. For Koba, when her tantrum passed, had obviously rushed back into Tapua village to pass on to the crew of the *Spindrift* the direction in which Culver was traveling through the hinterland. Behind her now came red-faced Burke, Birger Ukko, George Washington Green, Constantine, Alec, Will Carman, Sibu of Borneo, Latour, Francolini, and even old Peterson, the Negro cook. All the veterans of the *Spindrift* were there, ten men of almost as many nations, as hard a lot as one could pick up in a journey around the world.

Culver drew back a little. A weakening in his knees told him that he would have run for it if he had been alone; but Sally's presence chained him to the spot.

"Will they do you harm?" she asked. "I'll be safe with them if you want to take care of yourself."

He managed to twist a smile onto his lips. Then he leaned and opened the right hand of the dead man, still tightly closed. It was almost as warm and moist as life; and in the humid palm was a little globe of milky translucence.

He picked it up. The light in it watched him like an eye. It was one of those rare distillations of wealth. That was what gave it its soul, he thought. Imitations could be made

174

that looked exactly like it, and that would have to be tried on the teeth of the expert before they were known to be false. This was simply a freak of patient nature, worth because of its rarity, perhaps thousands and thousands of dollars, a pearl of large size and perfect roundness.

He showed the gem to the girl. "This is yours," he said. "Put it away."

They came on with hurrying strides, the men of the *Spindrift*. Burke shouted out something filthy and venomous from a distance; then he was at a halt near the dead man, and the rest of them banked up on either side of him, their hands helplessly swinging. For Napico, when he saw them coming, had planted himself between them and Culver. Now, leaning forward until the strain made the lead tremble, he begged with a high-pitched, constant snarling to be turned loose on them.

"Shoot the beast, and let's get our hands on Culver," said George Green.

Koba, at that, began to dance from foot to foot, springing up and down and pointing her slim brown arm at Culver.

"You see? You see?" she cried. "Oh, the lie in your belly, may it burn your heart now!"

Burke said: "You ratted on us, Culver. And by God, we're going to have the hide off you for it. What's happened here? Who shot this fellow? That's right, Ukko!"

"Look out!" cried Sally. "There's one behind you—turn around! Look out!"

"He's all right," answered Culver. "He's a friend to me."

Birger Ukko came up almost to the side of Culver. He stood there now with a little blunt-nosed revolver that seemed to have been specially made for his own short, compact inches. He waited in a silence, his slant, Oriental eyes surveying his shipmates watchfully. And they gave plenty of heed to him, for in a fight the Finn was proverbially deadly.

175

"What did they find is the main thing, not the skinning of Culver," suggested Alec. "Valdez gets this bird to guide him in; but what did he shoot him for, unless the brown fellow had seen more than was good for him to know?"

"They found so much," said Sally, "that they left this behind. Valdez left it behind, and went off with pocketsful of the rest. He couldn't bother to wait and make sure of everything."

She held out on the palm of her hand the big pearl. The sun struck it and filled it with light, until it grew larger than a moon in the eyes of the sailors. Big Burke groaned.

"Take after him, you fools!" he shouted at his men. "Why are you standing and looking? There's the way Valdez went!"

"How far would you stay on his trail without the dog to show you how?" demanded George Green, contemptuously.

"Lay forward with the dog, Culver!" commanded Burke. "Lay forward, man!"

"Beat him!" cried Koba, rather misunderstanding this talk. "You promised to beat him till he screamed, if you caught him—and here he is!"

"Wait a minute. Heave to! Hold on a minute," answered Burke. "The fact is that we need you, and you need us, Culver. I take it that this is Miss Franklin, that I saw in San Francisco; I take it that when you used the wireless that day to send a message, you were using it to send a call to her. Is that right?"

"That seems to be right," said Culver.

"You had to trick us," said Burke sadly. "You couldn't play a fair, open, sailorly game with us!"

This speech from Burke caused Culver to blink a little; and then, for all the simplicity of his nature, he could not help smiling a little.

Burke went on: "If you want to help her to her share of

176

what Toth got, how'll you ever twist it out of the hand of Valdez except with us helping. Don't that make sense to you?"

"Do you understand?" asked Culver, turning to the girl. He laid a friendly hand on Ukko's shoulder at the same time. The Finn looked down at the hand of Culver, and then back to his face, without expression. But it was plain that he had committed himself definitely to the side of Culver, in spite of the odds. "You understand?" repeated Culver.

When she was silent, watching him with an odd mingling of despair and amusement which he could not understand, he added to Burke: "I think it is time for us to unite our strengths. You have the hand power; we have the nose of the dog to find the way. But if we join you, will you promise that Miss Franklin shall have her proper half of whatever is recovered from Valdez?"

"Promise it? Of course I'll promise it!" growled Burke.

"And the rest of you?" asked Culver, in his quiet voice. "I think it might be a proper procedure to lift your right hands and swear to it."

"Leave me see what hand don't go up!" exclaimed Burke, looking savagely around him.

The sailors put up their hands. They seemed a bit shamefaced about it. But they all pronounced the two words.

"Get on, then. Get on, for God's sake!" called Burke, and Culver stepped out on the trail. For a moment Napico still lingered at his heels, half protesting, as though he felt these enemies to the rear needed more attention than the trail to the front; but presently he had forgotten everything except the scent, and was following it eagerly through the tall grass.

It was hard work almost from the start. On the outward journey Valdez had surrendered to the leadership of a guide, but for the back trip he apparently had trusted to

177

certain landmarks, or perhaps to an innate sense of direction. By this compass he steered a course which took him through heavy going a good part of the way. His enormous strides and leg power had taken him forward through heavy growth which flogged the body of Culver as he pressed on at the heels of the dog. Behind him came either Alec or George Green, who seemed rather at home in this sort of going. After them the way was fairly beaten down, and at the rear of the column came Sally and Koba.

The hot work put up the blood into the head of Culver, so that his thoughts came to him disjointedly; but he could not help wondering at the companionship which had been established between the two. Sally, struggling forward with her head more and more to one side as she grew exhausted, was being helped forward by the islander. And Koba had an excess energy for talking also. Once, as he looked back across a clearing before plunging at the heels of the dog into the green wall beyond, he recognized the gestures with which Koba told the tale of Jemmison, and the fall of the bosun, so that he could guess that the girl was telling once more the tale of the ship and the fighting of her "much man." And once again, as he came down a sharp slope just beyond sight of Tapua, he heard a sudden silver ringing of laughter behind him, and knew that the girls had struck upon something mutually amusing. Could the subject be he, again?

As he toiled up the next slope, his arms aching from holding the tireless horses that strained and charged in the body of Napico, he returned to the dreary thought that he never would understand the minds of the people around him. To the end of time they would be mysteries to him, he felt, and the wall of obscurity still would close him around to his dying day. So he would still remain a target for laughter; he would still be absurd, and never know what his own absurdities might be. So, as he walked on through the humid hot green behind the dog, he felt that untold leagues of distance were lengthening out between him and the girl. And then, coming over the next rise, he looked up, and saw that the town of Tapua was spread out neatly beneath him, and beyond it the blue peace of the lagoon with the reef marked in white like a scar across the face of it, and near the harbor entrance, its sails feebly taking the wind that was yet masked in the lee of the island, there still within the curve of the harbor's arm lay the *Spindrift,* making slowly toward the open sea!

CHAPTER 22

That took the weariness out of their bodies, you can be sure. The sailors broke past Culver and the dog, floundering ahead with great shouts. For they knew why the ship was sailing. They knew that Captain Valdez, having crossed the southern seas and caught up his prize, had found his own ship conveniently waiting for him in the harbor. No doubt he had learned that the tough old veterans of his crew were ashore. So, perhaps picking up a few hands in Tapua, he probably had rowed out to the *Spindrift* and boarded her as he had a legal right to do; and now, a bit short-handed but in perfect comfort, he had the way open to sail to any part of the world with his fortune.

What complaint could the others offer? If they tried to complain, they simply were accusing themselves of sea robbery in having stolen the ship; and another name for robbery at sea is piracy. Their hands were completely and

179

perfectly tied. The complete irony which underlay their situation overwhelmed them all. Even George Green forgot his sinister dignity to curse as he ran hopelessly forward. Little Sibu, in a catlike passion, ran forward, dropped to the earth to tear at the grass and beat the ground, then sprang up and ran ahead once more, like a rabbit running from the hounds. Burke, drunk with rage as with whisky, staggered as he ran.

Even Sally Franklin was crying out something about stopping the ship; but in what way could it be stopped? There was surely not a soul in the company who felt the slightest pleasure except Culver, alone. For two selfish reasons that shamed him, his heart was lightened. Wealth would only widen those leagues which already separated him from Sally Franklin; and on the ship was the master of Napico. The poor dog, struggling down-headed along the slope, pulling as violently as when the journey inland began, could not fit into his brute's mind the meaning of that distant picture of the ship that was departing. He could only know the scent which lay under his nose and which meant the road back to the master. But if he did not reach Valdez now, who could tell how long it would take before he began to be Culver's dog in fact?

So Culver, as he stumbled down the hill, took a grim comfort out of this moment. He permitted himself that selfish pleasure for a moment only. Then his better side began to assert itself.

Alec was shouting something about getting the tug and putting to sea after the old ship, before it found the wings of the trade wind and sailed off beyond their reach. There was a ghost of a hope in that. The sailors were well in the lead to rush after that chance, when Culver came down into the first street of the village with Sally. When he looked around, amazed, he saw that Koba had not come all the way with them. Instead, she stood on the verge of the inland wall of green, waving a hand and laughing. And somehow he knew that the anger was gone out of her, and that he was the subject of her mirth. Some secret, some absurdity about him, must have been imparted to her by Sally. For Sally also, turning to wave, was smiling in spite of her weariness.

They had not gone onward for five minutes before the frantic figure of Tommy Wiley came toward them, almost on a run. He was as red and sweating as though he had been a member of the party all day long. Where had they been, he wanted to know; and why was no message left for him? And again, with a furious look at Culver, where had they been? he demanded.

Sally answered him the most direct way by showing him the pearl in the palm of her hand.

"We've found the place," she said, "but Valdez apparently was there before us. We found his dead man, and one pearl, and—Help me, Tommy! Help me to catch up with the sailors! There's still half a chance that we can get out to sea and catch the *Spindrift* and that rascal and what's due to us."

That was sufficient explanation for Tommy Wiley. The three of them hurried toward the pier where the tug was fast—and to give them hope, smoke was floating lazily from its stack. Tommy told them, in broken words, what had happened to him during the day, and how he had talked everywhere to everyone without getting so much as a hint of Valdez. The name was known everywhere, but no one had laid an eye upon Valdez. So a queer hope came to Culver that, after all, the man he dreaded meeting might not be on board the *Spindrift* at that moment. And yet he knew, with a strange surety of the unconscious mind, a queer working of instinct, that he would find Valdez somehow, at the end of this trail. He could put his trust in Napico to that extent, at least.

They found a dense group of natives and a few non-descript whites gathered at the foot of the pier beside the tug to listen to the bargaining. Above other voices, that of Burke was shouting: "I'll tell you, man, that we'll pay you twice a hundred when we get out to the ship."

"Man and boy," answered a rolling bass voice, "I've followed the sea fifty years, and I've never seen a sailor that wouldn't be damned rather than pay a debt when he's off-shore."

"You fool!" shouted Burke.

"Ah, and I'm a fool now, am I? We'll just call it two hundred dollars that I want paid into my hand before I take off a line for you," said the captain of the tug.

He sat on top of the superstructure of the tubby little boat, smoking a pipe upside down, with a brimless hat stuck on the back of his head. He was gray and fat and sixty, a true wharf rat, and he seemed to enjoy this argument more than the hope of money. It seemed a bit strange to Culver that Burke and his men did not rush the tug at once and do as they pleased with the boat afterward. Perhaps the answer lay in the native stevedores and beachcombers who stood about, grinning. No doubt they were at the beck and call of the captain, and there were enough of them to throw the sailors into the sea. That might have explained the patience of Burke, whose face seemed red and swollen enough to explode, but who lifted his voice only to argue.

"We're robbed by the bloody captain! We're robbed by Valdez, and he's the father and the grandfather of all robbers!" shouted Burke. "Will you stand by if you're a sailor-man and see other poor devils robbed?"

"I'll have two hundred dollars before I can lift a line from the pier head," answered the captain, and took a long draw at his pipe.

182

"Oh, for the name of God and the mother of heaven!" groaned Burke. "Is there no man or mercy in the world that'll give me the money to pay this old devil, and let us get after a thousand times what he's asking?"

"Old devil, am I?" echoed the captain of the tug. "We'll call it an even three hundred, or there's not a line that I'll lift from the pier."

Burke, when this Pelion was piled upon Ossa, lifted both fists to the sky in wordless complaint and appeal.

"Have we that much, Tommy?" asked the girl.

"We have the tickets back and a hundred and fifty," said Tommy. "But we can't spend all—"

The *Spindrift* was standing well out now, toward the reef, nearing the verge of the smooth harbor water, though none of her sails were perceptibly filled by the breeze. She was, as the saying went on board the ship, holding her steerageway by the flap of her canvas. Just beyond her nose, she was pointing toward the darker blue of the open sea, roughened by a fresh wind. Once in that, she would be off like a gull and sail forever.

Culver said to the girl: "Let me have the pearl, if you please."

"Wait!" protested Tommy. "It looks like ten thousand dollars' worth of—"

But Sally already had passed the jewel without a word to Culver. He gave a strange look into her tired face as he took it. Then he stepped forward off the pier and over the gunwale of the tug, with Napico beside him.

The captain jumped down from the top to confront him.

"I'll have 'em break you in two and duck you to the bottom of the harbor!" he shouted at Culver.

"Look at this," said Culver, "and see if it's worth our trip out to the ship."

And he laid the pearl in the hand of the captain. Against

183

that calloused, grimy palm it shone with a peculiarly tender beauty and brightness. The captain gave it one look, then folded his pudgy grip over it.

"On board, then, all of you!" he shouted. "Cast off, Mickey! On board, on board! What are you hanging back there for, if you're so keen to go? If I won't take your money, maybe I'll take you for fun!"

He gave Culver a look. He was a much-changed man. And a moment later he was in his cabin at the wheel, sounding bells.

That was how they came to head across the lagoon with the sailors from the *Spindrift* clustered forward, eagerly reaching out after the prize with their hopes.

Burke got to Culver in a passion of gratitude. He said: "I'll be remembering this to the end of my days, Culver. There was the damned square-headed Dutchman, and there was me, and him like a fence in front, and me like a horse with the hobbles onto it. And Culver come and boosted me over. Look and listen to me, man. If there's nobody else that lays a hand on a bit of the stuff, except one, you're to be the man. May the mother that bore me, and the priest that blessed me, and—"

The coldly considering eye of Culver for some reason stopped this enthusiastic outbreak.

"Ah, man," said Burke, "you wouldn't be remembering old scores against a shipmate, would you?" And he hurried away forward to join the others.

Tommy Wiley was saying nervously to the girl: "But every stitch of everything we have, left back there to the cockroaches in Tapua—and what—"

"Hush, Tommy," said the girl.

She lay flat on her back on the afterdeck, which sat low down over the green combing of the wake. She had her eyes closed and her arms thrown out sidewise.

184

"Where is he?" she asked.

"Culver?" interpreted Tommy, frowning. "Why, he's standing here."

She did not open her eyes but held up one hand. Culver sat on his heels and took it.

"You didn't mind, did you?" she asked.

"Mind? I don't understand," said Culver.

"You didn't mind the laughing, did you?" she repeated.

"Your laughter and Koba's? Certainly not," said Culver. "It may have helped you through some of those last tired miles. Laughter, I believe," said Culver, "is in the nature of a narcotic; it relieves the tension of expectation and worry."

"Is there a good word among the poets about that?" she asked, with a smile trembling at the corners of her mouth, and going out again at once.

Still she did not look up at him; and the heart of Culver died in him as he saw that mockery hidden as it was about to appear. He put down his head a bit and considered. But all he knew how to do was to answer a question honestly, no matter how lightly it might have been asked. Then he was saying: "There is something in the poets, I dare say. Let me think. There is this, at least:

> Let not my ladder be her golden hair
> For climbing to her heart, but let it be
> Her sweet, clear laughter, like a winding stair.

"Ah, I like that," said Sally.

She was still, drawing deep breaths.

Then she said: "It was better to laugh and to have her laughing than to have her knife in your back, wasn't it, Samuel? Or better than to have her own heart broken, don't you think?"

He tried to follow this explanation, but found that it was

very difficult for him.

"Do you understand?" she asked.

"I hope that I shall," said Culver.

"Samuel," she murmured, "if you make me pity you, what shall I do? On top of all the rest, if you make me pity, won't I be lost forever?"

"Pity?" he echoed, deeply hurt. "I hoped that I hadn't deserved that!"

"Ah, don't you understand? Won't you understand?" she asked. "Tell me something, quickly, out of some tremendously great poet, as old as the neolithic age, at least—tell me something about misunderstanding. Please do!"

In his troubled mind he searched. "There is this, perhaps," he said at last, and quoted:

> I pray for dawn. The darkness is a sword
> That pierces me. I pray for heavenly light
> And truth that is the vision of the Lord.

"Tommy!" whispered the girl.

The tall lad came hurrying to her.

"Sit down beside me, please," she begged. "Stay close to me—I'm almost a thousand leagues away from you."

Culver stood up and stepped back from them, for he felt he was not wanted. And the first salty sea wind cut into his face with a familiar chill. They were rounding the reef now. The uproar of it was musical and surprisingly distant. He knew how those voices sounded when they were shouting at his ear. Narrowing his eyes, he could see, and only barely see, the little rift through which the sea had driven him to safety, beyond the reach of Jemmison's boat hook.

But the *Spindrift* was there on the starboard bow right ahead, her upper sails now filling, and her whole slender body giving gracefully to the wind as though she loved it. She was gathering speed, but the tug still was able to walk up on her, hand-over-hand. Burke made his men get out of view below, and he stowed himself with them.

"If Valdez sees my mug," he said, "there'll be general hell to pay before he ever lets us lay him aboard. But if he sees Culver and the girl and the young gent, why, he's never laid eyes on them before, has he? And besides, there's big Napico for him to spot from a long lookout, and that'll be the filling of his eye for him, damn his rotten heart!"

That was why the tug swept up toward the *Spindrift* with only Culver showing near the girl, and young Tommy Wiley aft on the boat, with Napico, already strangely excited, standing up with his paws on the rail.

"Ahoy the *Spindrift!*" shouted the captain of the tug. "Throw us a line, will you?"

"Ahoy the tug!" thundered a great voice that seemed to boom down out of the sky. "Keep away and give me sea room. Keep off!"

The voice came from the waist of the ship, a bit aft, toward the break of the poop; and something in Culver rose up to recognize the sound, as though it were something which he had heard in his dreams and had been waiting for. As for Napico, he whined with eagerness, and tried to climb right up on the edge of the rail. Then Culver saw the man who had spoken. He was standing near the rail, bareheaded, his long black hair whipped back from a head that was partly bald above the temples. It was the same profile Culver had seen—and never forgotten—on the night Napico came into his hands. But despite the ugliness of that great beak of a nose and the protruding chin, there was something distinguished in Valdez' look that saved him from the effect of perfect ugliness.

"Sheer off!" he thundered again, and the captain started turning the tug off its course. A groan from the men of the *Spindrift* who were under cover sounded like something gone wrong with the engine.

Then Valdez called out again: "Very well, come on alongside—long enough for me to get the dog on board. Lay close alongside, and you won't need a line, Captain. ↙ . . . Hai, Napico! Hai, Pico, my boy!"

Napico lifted his nose and howled into the wind with excess of joy.

Burke, from the after entrance of the tug's cabin, was saying:

"Wait till you see me start, and then go for the *Spindrift*. Swarm out and board her. Alec, you've got that boat hook. Bury it in the side of the *Spindrift* like you was lancing a whale, and pull us in close. And hold us there. God help us now—God help us, this is the pinch. Holy Saint Catherine, I promise twelve candles longer than my arm, and—"

"The dog comes on board, and nothing else!" hailed Valdez. "Mind, on board the tug. Nothing but the dog!"

He balanced a rifle in one hand, resting his elbow on the rail as he spoke. And the overtaking wind, increasing every moment, leaned the *Spindrift* with a sound of working gear alow and aloft. Pots and pans in the galley, for harbor usage unsecured, slid away to crashing fall.

Culver, looking up, saw only the face of Valdez, and felt only the tugging vibration of Napico on the lead.

"Hold onto the dog till we're close on board her," groaned Burke from the cabin. "Steady with the dog, Culver, and God be kind to you! Steady, Culver, and it's all in your hands to come in touch with him."

They were swinging close inboard now, with the burdened waist of the *Spindrift* not high above the level of the tug's rail.

"You there below—you on Napico's lead—let him come, now! And board us yourself, if you wish. I want to see the man who can handle that dog without a muzzle on him! What's your name?"

"Culver," he answered.

"Look alive, Culver! Let the dog go—now! And spring up yourself. I'll have a hand for you."

He stretched out his big right hand as he spoke. It was the arm and hand of a giant, and Culver looked on the gesture with awe. But he could not take advantage of a friendly proffer when he came as an enemy.

That was why he shouted: "Captain Valdez, if I come, it's not as a friend!"

"What's that?" called Valdez.

"Ah, God, the fool!" groaned Burke again. "Now out and at him, boys! Hearty, my lads! Out and swarm aboard him, and an extra share for him that puts lead in Valdez. Alec! Right on my heels, old Alec, and give the boat hook into the side of her—hard, hard!"

Culver heard the rush of feet behind him, and from the tail of his eye he saw them coming, Burke first, with a frantic, convulsed face of effort; and there Alec with the boat hook poised in both hands, and chunky little Birget Ukko next in order.

"Ah-ha?" cried Valdez. "Oh, my prophetic soul!"

And he jerked the rifle to his shoulder to fire. It was not intentional on the part of Culver to loose the big dog at that moment, but the shock of seeing the rifle at Valdez' shoulder had unsteadied him for an instant, and a lurch on the part of Napico whipped the end of the lead out of his hand. An instant later Napico was sailing straight for the arms of his master. His flying bulk knocked the rifle whirling to one side, so that it dropped into the sea after glancing off the bulwark of the tug. And as Alec drove home the boat hook, tying the ships together, the veterans of the *Spindrift* instantly swarmed aboard from the tug.

Culver, with his grasp on the *Spindrift's* rail, gave Sally a strong hand to help her on board. Tommy Wiley, as though he had forgotten her in the excitement, was already there. And Culver was literally the last man to gain the deck of the *Spindrift*. He was in time to see Burke and Birger Ukko open fire on a huge figure that leaped onto the poop and disappeared down the companionway of the after cabin. Napico followed.

"Follow him! After him, lads! Bring the old fox out of his hole!" roared Burke; and like a good leader, he headed the wave of shouting men who poured aft.

Culver, looking undeterminedly to the right and left, saw the tug sheer off, and watched its captain come out of his cabin, grinning broadly at the mischief which he was leaving behind him. Tom Wiley was already with the rush of the sailors who followed Burke. That, for the moment, left Culver alone in the waist of the ship with Sally Franklin, and he discovered that she was looking in that tense crisis not at the action around her, but intently, curiously, into his face. He half expected her to ask, as usual, what the poets could say at such a time as this. Then a gun barked twice, aft, and Burke jumped down the ladder to the deck, cursing and shaking his fist. Captain Valdez evidently had missed his head narrowly by firing from the top of the companionway into the cabin. The attack had been checked just when it seemed about to overwhelm everything in its first rush.

The ship, as Culver took stock of it, was divided roughly into three commands. Forward and in the rigging were the new hands, including the bosun and also including O'Doul, who was of the veterans; but O'Doul was now whizzing down a backstay to join the old company. The new hands did not stir to join the mutineers. Under the break of the poop were Burke and the rest; aft, there was no helmsman at the wheel, and Valdez apparently commanded the approaches to that deck.

The ship, swaying into the light wind, began to roll a bit in the swing of the waves, as brainless as an unmanned raft. If a squall should strike her now without a helmsman, the mischief might be quick and great. Whoever had the trick at the wheel had come forward during the excitement, and now the return was blocked. Instead of at the companionway's head, the Captain had now taken post at a small port which opened at the forward end of the poop deck, a litle round, single eye that commanded the whole sweep of the deck, and an unusual feature of the *Spindrift*.

He called out in his thundering voice from this place of vantage:

"Will you talk turkey now, Burke, and the rest of you? You poor devils, have you let Burke lead you into piracy, and now do you want to let him lead you into murder also?"

They shrank uncertainly from the voice and the gun of Valdez.

"Here's the time for a parley," he said; "who'll speak up for you, besides Burke?"

CHAPTER 23

During the small pause that followed, Culver noticed that more than one anxious eye turned not toward the Captain at the port, but upward toward the canvas which was slatting, and the spars jarring most unnaturally against the masts. He himself felt a distinct unease. They were in a ship without an acknowledged master, as though life were

191

in a body without a brain.

Burke sang out: "I'll talk for myself, and I'll talk for the others, Captain Valdez."

"I'll have no dealings with a mutineer and a ringleader," said Valdez. "I'll see the *Spindrift* go down and all hands aboard her, before I'll talk with Burke. . . . Keep forward there, Ukko! None of you try to sneak aft and get under the break of the poop. I'll wing you, my lads, if you try it!"

Sally said to Culver: "Tell me—are you afraid?"

"I'm sorry to say that I am," he answered. "Does it surprise you?"

She merely watched him, too intently curious to make an answer. It seemed to Culver that all the importance of this moment was somewhat less to her than the reactions she was studying in him.

"He'll talk to me, or he'll talk to nobody!" Burke was saying.

"Why bat your head against a wall?" asked the O'Doul. "Pick out another head, or a couple of them. Pick out George Green and another to talk to the Captain."

To the mutineers, this seemed good advice. Old Peterson, whose age and character gave immense weight to his words, remarked: "Why fight with your luck when you find it? Where would we be without Culver? Pick out Culver to go with George Green and talk to the Old Man."

They turned about and stared at Culver; and he stared back at them, surprised; but since Peterson had identified Culver with their luck, no one was of a mind to challenge the selection of him on the committee.

"Go aft, then," commanded Burke. "Go aft and show him that he's in our hands as neat as can be."

"Send some one aft, first, to man the wheel," suggested Culver.

"And get his head shot off by Valdez as he climbs over

the break of the poop?" asked Burke, sneering.

"Three or four men could drop over the rail and hand themselves aft," said Culver.

"Ay, and that's more than a fool's idea," agreed Burke. "Ukko and O'Doul and Sibu—you wildcat—go aft over the rail and man the wheel!"

They were over the side in a moment, only their hands flashing above the rail as they swung aft along the side of the ship.

Culver went under the little round port with its heavy concave glass behind which Valdez had posted himself.

He said: "Now that's a simple idea, but I didn't think that it would come to you lunkheads for a day or two at least—that idea of getting men aft to the wheel over the ship's side. Who thought of that?"

"The new hand, here. Culver thought of it," said Green.

"Ah, Jimmy," said the Captain, "you were right when you said that there was more to him than met the eye, and yet plenty meets the eye, at that. Culver, I'm glad to have you on shipboard. Now, my lads, what do you think of it all?"

"We have you up a tree, sir," said George Green.

"You'd like that, Green, wouldn't you?" asked Valdez, in his deep, rumbling voice. "I could always see the green in your eyes when my back was turned to you. I dare say that there never was a man born who was good enough to be captain over you, Green."

Green said: "We have you up a tree, sir, like a 'possum, and you'll never get away with the stuff you took from Walter Toth."

"Speaking of Toth," said the Captain, "how did you manage to lay such a close course for Tapua?"

"We picked your letter out of the basket," said Green, "and we laid it together, end for end, and made everything out; except we were wrong about the last paragraph, but

Culver set us straight there."

"Ah, Culver, I've heard about that," said Valdez. "First and last, you've been a useful fellow to them, haven't you?"

Culver said nothing, because he could think of nothing to say.

"Now, the way the matter stands is this," said Valdez: "You lads feel that you have me firmly in hand, and yet you ought to know that I've never been had in hand before, and it would be very strange if I cooped myself up here and let you hold the major cards. . . . Jimmy, how are we for water?"

"Water?" said the voice of the pseudo-chaplain from the background. "Why think of water, when there's plenty of wine?"

"How much water have we?" insisted the Captain.

"Call it thirty gallons," said Jimmy Jones.

"Call it thirty gallons," agreed Valdez genially. "And how do we stand for food?"

"The biscuits I won't count," said Jimmy Jones.

"No, don't count them. But the rest?"

"There are a few hams, and some dried beef, and about sixty cans of fish and meat," said Jimmy Jones.

"Good old Jimmy," said Valdez, "what a comforter you are in the pinches! Now my boys, your new commander, your Burke over there, very foolishly failed to provide a stock of fresh water and provisions the instant he reached Tapua. The result is that you'll all be on short rations within a month. Is that clear? You'll be starving yourselves while Jimmy and I and Napico live here on the fat of the land. In a word, the best thing for you to do is to put Burke in irons, come aft and pile your weapons, and remember that you're sailing before the mast with Captain Valdez, and ready to obey orders."

Green answered to this rather convincing remark: "We

can pick up chuck on the way."

"If you enter harbor," said Valdez, "I'll have you jailed as mutineers and hanged afterward for piracy."

"If we enter harbor," argued Green, "how would you let 'em know, on shore, that there's any trouble on board, if we have you cooped up under deck?"

"You can keep me cooped, but you can't coop up red fire, Green," said Valdez. "With a wind aft, what an easy trick it would be, as we entered harbor, to throw out a supply of oiled oakum and papers onto the deck and let the flames blow forward? Tarred rigging burns fast, Green, and there soon would be a fine tower of jewels for the people on shore to look at. When they came off in boats, a few score of them, what a simple matter for me to come up with Jimmy Jones and Napico, and be rescued with the rest of you!"

There was a silence. Then Valdez added: "You see, Green, I've thought the matter out before I consented to retire below deck. I have no objection to resting here in comfort while you go forward and convince the rest of your shipmates that you never can make a harbor while I'm aboard her; and if you do, I'll slip out of your hands first, and have you hanged afterward. Ay, rub your neck, Green. Stimulate the flow of blood to the brain, but you'll never get past that idea. Facts are hard things to swallow, my lad, but sometimes swallowed they must be."

Green looked hopelessly at the deck, then up into the top-hamper, where the sails were filling pleasantly as the helmsmen brought the ship into the wind. The *Spindrift* was finding her sea legs again.

"Mutiny and piracy—" he murmured, and ran the red tip of his tongue over his lips. It was plain that the two terms daunted him a good deal.

At last he broke out: "We can rush the companionway

and get down and smoke you out, then!"

"I think you might," agreed the Captain. "But I don't think you would. You know that Jimmy Jones only claims one virtue in the world, and that is the virtue of shooting straight. I would be here with him, and the third of us would be Napico, who carries teeth that some of you ought to remember. No, no, Green: you'll not be rushing the companionway for a long time. But if you did, and if you were winning, by God, the pearls would go into the sea before I'd have them taken away from me by a mutinous crew. You know me, Green. The others know me also. You understand that I'm telling you the truth. Your hands are tied behind you, my lad. . . . But I'll tell you what I'll do: For Burke in irons and the weapons piled aft, here under my eyes, I'll give to every member of the old crew one beautiful large pearl worth ten long voyages, at least. I'll give them ten or twenty years' pay in a lump. You see, Green, I've no idea of cheating people; but I don't want to give away more than proper rights."

He said these things slowly, pausing in his phrases as an actor pauses when he wishes to give the effect of great sincerity and a searching of the heart.

Green said to Culver: "I guess it's right. At sea, he'll starve us out. On shore, we'll be hanged for piracy! There's no answer."

"There is only one, I think," said Culver. "If we go ashore, we can have him put under arrest for murder in Tapua."

"I'd forgotten that," said Green. He exclaimed: "We have you there, Captain!"

"And as for the countercharge," said Culver, "the charges made by a man under arrest for murder are not very seriously considered by the laws of any land, I believe. I don't believe that the crew of the *Spindrift* would be very seriously

196

bothered."

"Do you hear that, sir?" cried Green. "I guess we have you on that count, eh?"

He laughed with relief and happiness. The black eyes of Valdez dwelt earnestly on the face of Culver as he answered: "Jimmy Jones was right. He is always right. You are unusual, Culver. . . . But as for murder in Tapua: if someone was found dead there, might he not have been murdered by the crew as well as by the Captain? However, I'm a fellow who believes in bargaining. I think it's only fair to say that. And I think that we could come to a very amicable agreement here. Suppose that you let Mr. Culver come into the cabin and talk matters over with me quietly and man to man. Wouldn't that be better in the long run?"

"Maybe it would," said George Green. "There's nothing lost trying, and he seems to know the answers."

Culver went back with Green to the others. The voice of Valdez had been heard by them all. Burke was pale with anger and with fear.

"Irons?" he said. "Irons is what he wants for me, is it?"

"Do you dare to go down to him, alone?" the girl asked Culver.

"I hardly dare, and yet it seems that I must go," he answered. "Ukko, can you lend me that gun of yours, in case there is an argument which goes beyond words? But no, if I had the gun, I would hardly know how to use it, and it's better to use talk only."

"Do you mean that you're going with only your bare hands? You can't do that!" cried Sally. "There's no trust to be put in him!"

"Perhaps there is not," answered Culver, sighing; "and yet there is nothing to do but go back to him. So good-by for a moment, Sally."

He turned about on his heel and walked rapidly aft, leaving a silence behind him. He could not help remembering that prophecy of Birger Ukko, long days before, when he said that someone was about to die on board the *Spindrift*. That prophecy was still unfulfilled, and Culver had a chilly sense that its fulfillment might not be far away. Behind him he heard Sally crying out to the other men: "Don't let him go! You can see what Valdez wants. He hopes to get Culver away from you because he's afraid of his hands and his brain. Don't you see that?"

The least voice from any of the men would have stopped Culver readily; but no one sang out after him, not even Birger Ukko, who had proved on Tapua that he was willing to die with his friend. And the feet of Culver carried him on unhappily, step after step, up the ladder to the poop and across the raised deck, and then down the companionway; and still the only voice that was raised to stop him was the last cry from the girl. He had another line from the poets to fortify him as he went down the inner steps:

> Outcast by men, outcast from all their ways
> And like a child left to the hands and talk
> of women—

One word from any of the men could have stopped him, but the pity of a woman was not enough. So he came down to the cabin door and stood for a moment in doubt.

Jimmy Jones, forward at the end of the passage, from which he looked out toward the waist with a short-barreled shotgun in his hands, turned to say: "Go right in, Culver. Go right in. The Captain is waiting for you. I've given you quite a name with him."

So Culver pressed down on the handle and stepped into the cabin of Valdez. The man loomed in the farther corner, looking almost as tall as the ceiling. As the door closed and the latch clicked behind Culver, Valdez said quietly, "Take him, Pico!" and at the same time lifted an old-fashioned single-action revolver, fired by working the hammer with the thumb.

Perhaps Pico had been trained to take people by the legs, giving them the weight of his shoulder to knock them sprawling so that his teeth could be at the throat an instant later. That was what Valdez must have expected. Even Culver was amazed when the huge dog, instead of jumping to the attack, reared up with a whine of welcome and placed his forefeet against Culver's chest. . . . The bullet from Valdez' gun drove the head of the dog heavily against Culver.

"Pico!" Valdez cried out, as the dog dropped. He lowered the gun as he shouted, and in that instant Culver was across the cabin floor. His shoulder slammed Valdez back against the wall with a force that shook the whole room. His left hand got the gun; then the fist of Valdez smashed across his jaw with a resistless sway like the brazen knuckles of a walking beam. The blow knocked Culver slithering to his knees and halfway back to the door. Through a fog he saw Valdez striding toward him, and into the midst of that dimness he fired the gun as his eye had seen Valdez do, lifting the hammer with the thumb.

The mist remained, but there was no Valdez looming in it. Culver wiped a hand across his eyes and stood up. Valdez was there on the deck, face down, with one huge hand reaching out almost to Culver's feet.

"Valdez! Valdez!" called Jimmy Jones. "Is it over, Diego?"

Culver turned the lock in the door.

CHAPTER 24

He turned Valdez on his back. The eyes of the Captain were wide open and filled with intelligent life.

"All right, Culver," said Valdez. "You held the aces, this time. Extraordinary that the cards you held should have been Napico. Will you take a look at the poor devil and see if he's quite done for?"

Culver stepped back, still with his eyes on the Captain and the gun raised.

"Don't worry about me," said Valdez. "I'm done for. I have it. It was a bull's-eye, my friend. . . . But tell me about Napico."

Culver kneeled by the dog and felt for the heart. His eyes refused to dwell on the great red gash across the head, for when he looked at it, he could feel the shock of the bullet striking his own flesh, as it were, and tearing through his body, flesh and bone. To his bewilderment, he found that the huge beast's heart was still beating, rapidly and surely.

"There's still life in him, Valdez!" he said.

"Is there?" asked Valdez. "Now, thank God for that! I've cheated him out of a good deal; I'm glad that I haven't cheated him out of his life."

"Valdez! Valdez! Diego, is it finished?" called the voice of Jimmy Jones, closer to the door.

"Let him in, will you?" asked Valdez.

Culver hesitated. When he saw the red spot which was forming across the breast of Valdez, he felt that he could not refuse the request of a dying man; and yet he had al-

200

ready heard that Jimmy Jones was a real man with a gun.

Valdez read his mind.

"Take the gun away from Jimmy," he said. "There's nothing to fear from him, the moment he sees me like this. Let him come in and leave the gun outside."

Culver unlocked the door, set it slightly ajar.

"Put down the shotgun, Jones, if you please," said Culver. "Captain Valdez is injured, and wants you to come in."

The gun crashed from the hands of Jimmy Jones to the deck. Jimmy Jones came running, his eyes and mouth wide open like those of an astonished child, and his short legs waddling under the fat of his belly. He squeezed through the door past Culver and fell on his knees beside his friend. He kept making the face of one who screamed at the top of his lungs, but all that came from his throat was a whispering voice that said over and over: "Diego! Diego!"

"Stop moaning and yammering," answered Valdez. "There's nothing to do. I have it, Jimmy. Right through the middle of the sentence. Hold up my head. I don't want to die flat on my back like a woman!"

Jimmy Jones squatted cross-legged and took the head of Valdez in his lap.

"The blood will get all over you, and you'll hate that," said Valdez. "But stay there like a good fellow, even if I make a sloppy mess, will you?"

"You have something here that I came to talk about," said Culver.

"Ah, that stuff?" answered Valdez. "It's over there in the chamois bag, in the drawer of the table."

Culver opened the drawer, accordingly, and took out a small chamois bag. He pulled open the mouth of it and looked down into a great double handful of pearls, every one a chosen masterpiece of nature, and the whole as dimly luminous in the bag as a cluster of moons behind a sea mist.

201

He wedged the sack down into his pocket.

In this manner the work of Walter Toth was completed. . . .

"Five minutes ago," said Valdez, "that little sack was worth more to me than anything in the world—always excepting you, Jimmy."

Tears ran unregarded down the fat cheeks of Jimmy Jones. He drew in a long, sobbing breath, but said nothing.

"And now," said Valdez, "it holds so many bright little pebbles. I feel enormously wise, Culver; out of this magnificent hour I could deliver enough moral sentiments to restock the world if Confucius were erased from every book. . . . Reach me a bottle of brandy from that cupboard, like a good fellow. The short, pot-bellied bottle. That, at least, is real Napoleon. Perhaps the same vintage that the Little Corporal sipped after Austerlitz to take the cold out of his blood. Or perhaps he had it before Waterloo, when his stomach was behaving almost as badly as mine does now. . . . How kind of you, Mr. Culver!"

For Culver had found the bottle, which was open and a third gone. He filled two glasses, offering one to the dying Captain and the other to Jimmy Jones.

"I can't take it. I won't take it!" groaned Jimmy.

"What?" exclaimed Valdez softly. "Not drink a stirrup cup with me?"

"A stirrup cup—ah, God!" said Jimmy Jones. "You are leaving me, Diego!"

"It won't be long," said Valdez calmly. "Unless you stop leaning so hard on the port, it won't be very long before you wash yourself out to sea and follow me, Jimmy. I drink to better luck than that!"

They both drank, and Culver refilled the glasses. He thought of the crew gathered forward in the waist, growing more curious as time went on, perhaps. And he remem-

bered now with a peculiar sweetness the voice of the girl—
the voice that had called after him.

A groan that seemed human sounded from near the door.
Napico stood up weakly, and shook his head, sending the
blood flying in a fine shower. He went on uncertain feet
toward his master and sat down beside Valdez.

The Captain put his hand on the head of Pico, avoiding
the edges of the wound.

"Why, it's only a touch—a mere glancing blow—a little
memento," said Valdez. "But it moves you, doesn't it, Culver, to see the poor big dog at the side of his dying master?
Brings a tear to the eye, I should venture to hope. A scene
like this would quite gag a moving-picture audience, I
think."

"I dare say it would," said Culver. "I'm not familiar with
those performances, however."

"Aren't you? I think I see an envy in your eye, Culver,
as you look at me and the dog. In reward for this excellent
brandy, suppose I tell you how I won his love and how
you could win it after me."

"I should be very happy to learn," said Culver. "There
is some poet who says:

> I would not go in glory and in robes
> But only where love leads me by the hand.

"You love the big fellow, do you?" asked Valdez, squinting his eyes.

"Perhaps love is not too exaggerated a word," agreed
Culver thoughtfully.

"Honest," decided Valdez, "as honest as a lion, and yet
with some of the fox in you too. You would take some
knowing, Mr. Culver. I was a very foolish fellow to try to
get at the heart of the matter with a bullet out of a gun.
And yet if Napico had not come in the way, the whole ques-

tion might have been settled quite a long moment ago. I could see that you were putting a man's wise head on that great foolish child, my crew. But to come back to Napico: Shall I tell you how I mastered him?"

"If you please," answered Culver, and drew a little closer. Valdez smiled at this intense interest.

"We had touched at Juneau," he said; "and while I was on shore, I saw five dogs jump a big Mackenzie River husky. The husky rose up out of the heap with hardly a mark on him. Three of the other dogs were able to run. So I talked to his owner, who was standing by admiring, and found out that the dog was a touchy devil, perfect on the trail, but a murderer otherwise, and wild as a wolf. That combination spoke to me, Culver. Napico's master had not the slightest idea how to get even a muzzle on him. He would stand for sled harness, but nothing else.

"So I got four sailors with ropes, and after I'd bought the dog we managed to bring him on ship. I turned over that bunk cabin of mine to him, and fine hell he raised in it for a time. But thirst weakened him, and then I came as the savior, with water. He turned into a devil again. Once more starvation and thirst weakened him, and again I was the savior. I burned him with acid; and then I healed him with salves. I had him wounded, and I nursed him back to life. I gave him stuff that nearly ate the lining out of his belly, and then I gave him soothing oils and brought him back into shape again. It took me six months. He was a starved and staggering wreck before the end of it, but by that time he'd learned to wait for my step and listen to my voice. . . . And there you have him now, the picture of devotion, into which he was cheated. And having been cheated once, you, if you are patient enough, can cheat him again. . . . That's a fair return for the brandy, isn't it?"

"I could never do it," said Culver.

"Ah, you couldn't?" asked the Captain. "You wouldn't

buy the poor devil's heart with pain—is that it?"

Culver was silent.

"Well, well," said the Captain. "There is more and more to you. May I ask how the devil you knew that I had one dead Tapuan to my account?"

"Napico led me to the place," said Culver

"That was not difficult. As a matter of fact, I found that Toth in drawing the little chart of the way for you, had left an impression on the next page in the calendar."

"And you found that?"

"By holding each page in turn so that the light struck it slantwise. I have worked a good deal with books," explained Culver.

"So I see," said Valdez. "Not all lion," he murmured, "but partly fox. I guessed that almost from the first. . . . Jimmy, I'm growing a little weary. And I'm already old. Perhaps it was better to snuff out when there were still feet under me and hands to work with."

"Hush, and be still, Diego," said Jimmy Jones. "Or think of God and your sins!"

"Do I hear you naming God with a trembling voice, Jimmy?" asked Valdez. He smiled, but the color was leaving his face now. His swarthy skin turned a yellowish gray, his lips a pale purple.

"As for my sins," said Valdez, "they either are over my left shoulder, or else they are quite strong enough to sink me to the bottom of the sea. And as for God, if He sees me dying, He won't be fooled if he sees me scared into a few prayers at the last minute."

"Ah, but repentance, Diego—" groaned Jimmy Jones.

"What the devil should I repent?" asked the Captain. "Should I repent the free fine life we've lived on the ship? Should I repent the sweet hell that you and I have walked through? Should I repent the beautiful old *Spindrift?* If we've used her to smuggle a bit of an opiate, now and then, we've only given the world sweet dreams. And that's to the right side in our account. No, no, Jimmy, I'll die as I lived—" Here his breath shortened, and he gasped.

Culver, deeply moved, dropped to his knees and put his arms under the shoulders of Valdez.

"If I lift you, can you breathe better, Captain?" he asked.

"A little better," said Valdez, and Culver raised him somewhat.

Napico, as though he understood that help was being given, began to whine and lick alternately the cheek of Valdez and that of Culver.

"I give him to you, with my heart," said Valdez. "Be kind to him. No, I understand that you'll be that."

"Is there no man or woman in the world to whom I can take word of you?" asked Culver.

The Captain had closed his eyes, his body trembling with the pain that gripped him. Now he looked up, slowly, and regarded Culver with a smile in his misty eyes.

"Lion, fox and fool, in about equal parts, I'm afraid," he said. "I leave nothing behind me, Culver, nothing except the *Spindrift* and Napico. And so perhaps you'll be the master of them both. Who knows? But as for men and women, there's only poor, soggy, damned, desperate Jimmy Jones."

At this, Jimmy Jones broke into violent sobs.

"Don't do that," cautioned Valdez. "You're raining tears all over my face. Touching, Jimmy, very touching—but damned inconvenient! Let me die as dry as possible—except for my own blood . . . except for my own blood."

He was about to speak further; but when he had parted his lips, his mouth remained open and the word unspoken. His eyes closed.

"He's gone!" said Jimmy Jones. "Oh, God, he's gone, and I'm alone in the world! Oh, God—oh, God, what shall I do?"

206

It had seemed to Culver, also, that the last moment had come; but Valdez moved his lips to whisper. Napico on one side bowed his head close to listen, as though he were trying to catch a last soft command; and on the other side, Culver pressed his ear close.

"Be a little kind—to poor, poor Jimmy, will you?" whispered Valdez—and died. There was only a slight shudder of the legs and body, but Culver knew that the big man was gone.

CHAPTER 25

Afterward, Culver and Jimmy Jones staggered up the companionway with the dead body and laid it on the poop. Instantly the voice of the lookout shouted from high above: "On deck, there! Valdez is lying dead as a rat on the poop! Valdez is dead!"

Other voices started shouting. Culver went to the break of the poop and held up a hand that checked the rush of feet aft.

"I told you it was a gunshot!" someone was shouting, triumphantly. "Ay, ay, Culver! Good work old son!"

"Keep forward for a moment," said Culver. "It's true that Valdez is dead. Is there a man here to say a service over him before he's buried over the side?"

"The pearls! The pearls!" shouted Burke. "What in hell are you yammering about Valdez for? Where is Toth's stuff?"

"Safely put away," said Culver. "Where it will be divided in two halves when we reach San Francisco. One half to the old crew, and one half to Miss Franklin, as Toth provided. . . . Wiley, come aft to me. Sally Franklin, come with him. . . . Burke, will you make the bargain and hold to it?"

There was such an outcrying of many voices and such a trampling of feet as the new hands rushed back from the forecastle into the waist to hear more about this strange news, that for a moment there was no reasonable response.

Wiley and Sally Franklin, unhindered, climbed up to the poop. They stopped at the sight of the dead body, the dog and Jimmy Jones crouched beside it.

The girl said in a queer, pinched voice, like a child about to cry: "What have you done? What have you done?"

"Take her below. Take her down into the cabin," Culver directed Wiley.

Then he made out the bawling voice of Burke, calling: "What sort of a bargain is that? You keep the stuff till we make the harbor, and then how do we know that you'll split up fair?"

"The question, as it seems to me," said Culver, "is a fairly simple and unfortunate one: Are we to trust you if you once have everything in your hands, or are you to trust me? I can't help feeling that it would be safer for you to trust me."

"I'll trust nobody," said Burke, bellowing with anger. "You've seen what happened to Valdez when he tried to hold out!"

George Green remarked: "He was what happened to Valdez. Take a fresh hold on yourself, Mister. Culver wouldn't know how to cheat. He's our luck, isn't he? Answer up, lads. Is he the luck of the *Spindrift*.

They picked the question up and answered with a sudden heartiness, shouting: "Ay, ay! He's our luck. We'll stand by him."

208

"Let it stick that way, then," said Burke. "And be damned to the whole lot of you if it pans out wrong."

"There's a man up here that needs burial. Will you look to that, Burke?" asked Culver.

"Why not?" answered Burke. "I know the place in the book; and what's more, I've read it before."

He called out an order to the boatswain to get the body and prepare it for the sea.

Culver stepped aft to the dead man, the dog and Jimmy Jones.

He said: "Stay with him to the finish, Jimmy Jones. After that, come aft when you please. We'll try to make you at home there. If there's any way of doing it, I'll try always to give you a hand."

Jimmy Jones looked vaguely up at him, sighed and resumed his contemplation of the dead face.

"Here, Pico," called Culver. "Will you come with me, boy?"

The dog looked up, hesitated, then ran to Culver at the head of the companionway and paused there, glancing back toward his dead master.

Culver lifted him bodily and put him down on the top step. There they sat listening to the rising noise of the wind as it sang in the rigging, and the sloshing of the waters down the side of the ship. Napico made vague, half-hearted efforts to escape from Culver from time to time, but surrendering at last to the pain of his wound, he laid his head on Culver's knee and was quiet. And then, well forward, Culver heard the heavy splash and plumping sound for which he had been waiting. . . .

He stood up and went down into the cabin at once.

It was coming on toward sunset, and the cabin was a dull, rosy glow of light and trembling shadow. Young Wiley came to Culver from the open door of the little side cabin where Valdez kept his bunk.

He whispered: "She's in there, waiting for you. She's through with me. She loves you, Culver. Go in to talk to her."

He tried to step past, but Culver put out a hand and caught hold of him.

"Wait!" he whispered.

His understanding was trying to overtake the emotion that had broken over him like a combing wave. The white set face of young Wiley was giving him meanings out of the future, but he could not decipher them any more than he would have been able to understand a radio code message.

Gradually he broke down the code, so to speak, and arrived at a meaning.

Is there not the poet who sings:

> Darkness walls in the soul; man is not seen
> Save in the lightning flashes of his deeds.

So the girl had seen him, by flashes, enacting great things, or things great in meaning to her. And so, perhaps, she had been blinded by actions.

The heart of Culver ached. It seemed to him that if all the pearls had been moons indeed, and heaped before him as treasures, the value would be less than that happiness which waited for him in the next cabin, almost in touching distance; and then he remembered the years, and her youth; and his will, long tempered by pain and abstinence, steadied. There should be some way of putting her from him forever. That would be the mercy and the kindness. He remembered that pride is our strongest passion.

Still holding Wiley's arm he turned to him a face of such suffering as that lad had never seen before. But the voice with which he spoke was loud and ringing with a calm assurance.

"Stay here with the girl, Tommy," he commanded. "She's

tired out. There's not much strength in her. She's soft in the body, and I'm afraid there's not much mind-stuff in her to rescue her in a pinch. Treat her like a sick child, however, and she'll gradually rally. . . . I have other things to do, and can't waste time on her."

He had said it loudly. He saw a staggered comprehension in the face of Wiley, and then turned past him and went quickly out of the cabin, up the companionway, to the fresh wind on the deck. The sun was already half beneath the rim, puffing out its upper cheeks; and in another moment it was gone. The brief tropical twilight lasted only a moment, and there was a sense of the horizon closing in, like falling walls.

He stood by the windward rail, watching the stars come out beyond the wavering bows of the *Spindrift*.

Someone came up behind him and stood quietly in the lee he made. That was Jimmy Jones.

Forward, he could hear the men singing and he felt a brief longing for the forecastle and a return to the first frightened days when the ship was new to him, even when he still was seeing it through the fog of his weakened eyes. They were no longer weak. He was seeing more clearly. It seemed to Culver that the sight he had gained was too clear, both within and without. . . . He thought of the girl below, of her shame, the closed eyes of her agony of shame, having heard him speak. He thought of Tommy Wiley sitting by like one in fear, but waiting in hope also. He prayed that he had done the only thing that was honorable. And he wished that honor could be a kinder feeling in the heart.

He had a sense of inevitable return, now, to the old days, and he could not be sure that he would be glad to enter them. The days that had housed him in a sort of innocent sufficiency then might not be ample enough for him since he had sailed on the *Spindrift* and become, as the sailors put it, her luck. He felt that the sea, in a sense, had claimed him; and the faces of his books were dim in his mind, like half-remembered friends.

Something cold and moist touched the palm of his hand; Napico was there, looking forward down the curving length of the ship. He did not brace himself amply for the heeling of the ship and the pressure of the wind, but leaned heavily against Culver. A dollop of flying spray came inboard and struck the dog, and he looked up with a faint whine to the face of his friend. It was not a very great sign—but Culver knew that he had become the second master.